The next morning, Kasri made her way through the halls of Ironcliff. Though technically a city, the vast majority of it tunnelled into the side of a mountain, leading to corridors instead of streets, but to one of the mountain folk, it was all one and the same.

She slowed as she neared the doors to Agramath's study. Outside stood a member of the Hearth Guard, her own company of elite warriors, but all he did at her approach was nod in recognition.

"Is Lord Agramath within?" she asked.

"He is, Commander," replied the guard. "Along with the Human spellcaster. Shall I announce you?"

"If you would be so kind. Please ask him if he's available to speak with me at this time."

The guard cracked open the door and slipped inside. Moments later, he opened it fully, allowing her passage.

"Kasri," called out a voice. "So nice to see you again."

"Lady Aubrey, you grace us with your presence. I assume nothing is amiss in Wincaster?"

"Not at all. Master Bloom brought me to Ironcliff to commit the magic circle to memory. I was just making the necessary arrangements with Master Agramath."

"To which I have readily agreed," added the master of rock and stone.

"And Master Revi Bloom?"

"He left earlier this morning," said Aubrey.

"But you didn't come here to talk to her," said Agramath.

"How did you know?" replied Kasri.

"The surprise on your face."

"You have me there. I'll admit I knew she was in Ironcliff, but I didn't know she'd be here with you at this particular moment."

"If there's a problem," said Aubrey, "I can give you some privacy?"

"No, it's rather fortuitous you're here. I've got a little favour to ask."

"Which is?"

"I need to go to Wincaster."

"Need?" said Agramath. "Or want?"

"A little of both, I suppose. It's not official, just personal."

"Really?" said Agramath, eyeing her suspiciously. "What's that mean?"

"It's none of your business."

Also by Paul J Bennett

INTO THE FORGE

Mercerian Tales

Heir to the Crown
Book 10.5

PAUL J BENNETT

First Edition: October 2022

ePub ISBN: 978-1-990073-58-8
Mobi ISBN: 978-1-990073-59-5
Smashwords ISBN: 978-1-990073-60-1
Print: 978-1-990073-57-1

This book is a work of fiction. Any similarity to any person, living or
dead is entirely coincidental.

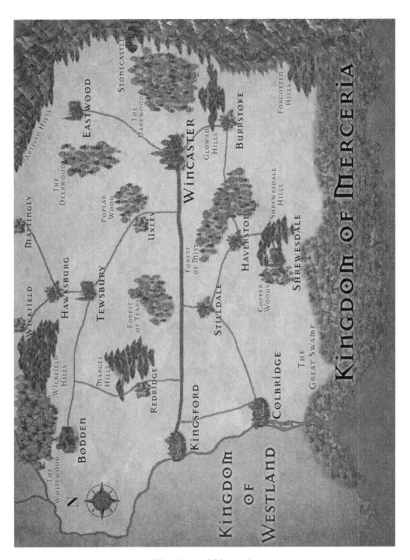

Kingdom of Merceria

Dedication

To my wife, Carol.

You are the wind beneath my wings

ONE

The Halls of the Vard

AUTUMN 966 MC* (*MERCERIAN CALENDAR)

(In the language of the Dwarves)

In Ironcliff, a champion lives,
A warrior, brave and true.
One Kasri Ironheart by name,
A hero through and through.

A daughter of the king was she,
Successor to the Throne.
A noble heart, a righteous foe,
Yet she was all alone.

The master of revels, Malrun Bronzefist, stood on the right side of the dancers, his free hand holding the great staff signifying his status. It was an honour to lead the dance on behalf of Vard Thalgrun, even more so on the occasion of his daughter, Kasri Ironheart, returning from the war.

Malrun rapped the floor ever so lightly, just enough to draw attention, then raised his staff, signifying the dance was about to begin. With all eyes on him, he brought it down again, thumping its base, signalling the musicians to play their instruments.

As was usual amongst the Dwarves of Ironcliff, drums tapped out the three-step beat common for such occasions, accompanied by a harp and even a few flutes.

Malrun's left hand grasped the vard's, while Thalgrun held his daughter's hand in his other. She held, in turn, the hand of the next person and so on, forming a line that stretched all the way to the side of the great hall.

The music swelled, and then with the introductory refrain complete, the dancers moved, taking two light steps, followed by a third to stomp their feet, the sound echoing off the massive walls.

The master of revels risked a sideways glance, noting the look of enjoyment on the vard's face. Long had it been since Vard Thalgrun displayed such joy, and why not? It wasn't every day his daughter returned fresh from victory and with a dragon, no less!

Malrun's musings almost cost him his dignity as he missed the beat, stumbling to catch up. He held his staff aloft in his attempt to recover, pretending it was all part of the merriment.

.   .   .

When the music subsided, Kasri immediately released her grip on her fellow dancer. With less than a third of the mountain folk female, many of the males waited off to the side, their beards bouncing around in time with the music. Before she could even catch her breath, a well-dressed Dwarf presented himself.

"Ah, Kasri," he said. "It is so wonderful for you to bless us once again with your presence."

"Thank you," she replied. "Graldur, isn't it?"

The fellow bowed deeply. "That would now be Deputy Guild Master Graldur of the mining guild."

"Congratulations, Deputy Guild Master." She tried to turn away from him, but he was insistent, even going so far as to touch her hand.

"Might I enquire if you would be interested in dining with me?"

"You may, but I'm afraid you would not like the reply. Now, if you're finished with my hand, I have need of it."

Her response was not what Graldur expected, for he stood there with his mouth hanging open. Before he said more, Kasri grabbed the vard by the elbow.

"Come, Father. There are things to discuss."

Vard Thalgrun, sensing her mood, left the dance floor but then halted, turning to face her. "Are you certain that was wise? Graldur is influential and not someone to anger."

"He wishes to forge with me," she replied. "He's made that quite clear on several occasions."

"And what is wrong with that? He's wealthy and influential, a prime catch by any measure. I daresay half the females here would be pleased to receive such attention."

"But not me. Isn't that what you were going to say?"

"Let's not have this discussion again, Kasri. You need to forge, if only to continue the line."

"Continue the line? You hand-picked me as your successor —the fact I'm your daughter wasn't even considered; at least that's what you told me. Are you now suggesting otherwise?"

"No, of course not. I selected you because you would uphold the virtues and ideals I espouse. You are also one of the few who command the respect of the warriors guild."

"Then why is it so important for me to forge?"

"We are not a populous people, my dear, as well you know. It, therefore, falls to those such as yourself to provide us with future generations."

"Because I'm a female? You do realize it takes two to procreate?"

Her father blushed. "I'm fully conversant with Dwarven reproduction, but you're the one who refuses to forge, despite my best efforts. Why, you could have your pick."

"And you feel Deputy Guild Master Graldur is a suitable match?"

"At this point, I'd be satisfied with anyone."

Kasri's sudden smirk put him ill at ease.

"What are you smiling at?" he asked.

"I'm merely soaking in your wisdom, Father."

The vard grunted. "Well, I suppose there's a first time for everything. How were things in Merceria?"

"Quite enlightening. They lack the heavy armour we take for granted, but you already knew that from their visit here."

"Yet I sense there's more to this tale. You came back with a dragon, although I wish you'd kept it here, in Ironcliff. It would help keep the Halvarians at bay."

"I could not," said Kasri. "I promised Melathandil she could live in the mountains. I believe you once told me a Dwarf is only as good as their word?"

"So I did, although I never thought you'd use it against me." He fell silent a moment as he stared into her eyes. "You're hiding something."

Kasri quickly looked aside. "What makes you say that?"

"Come, now. You think after all these years I can't tell when my own daughter is lying?"

"I'm not lying."

"Perhaps not, but you're not exactly telling the truth, at least not the entire truth."

She cast her gaze around the room, trying to avoid answering. The master of revels had once more lined up guests for a dance, even as the musicians picked up their instruments.

"Very well. I shall tell you what's on my mind, but not here. It's much too public."

"So now you tempt my curiosity? Have you no shame?" He smiled to lessen the blow. "Very well. Come see me tomorrow morning, and we shall discuss the matter in private, whatever it is."

Kasri bowed. "As you wish, Father."

"Now, will you join me once more on the dance floor? I hear the guild master awaits?"

"I think you mean the deputy guild master. I shall let you

have that pleasure all to yourself. I have more important business to attend to."

"You do? Like what?"

"I need to speak to Agramath about something."

"You'll have a hard time getting in to see him," said the vard. "He's meeting with one of those Mercerian mages."

"He is? Which one?"

"A Human woman. I don't remember her name."

"Not Albreda?"

"No, of course not. Do you honestly believe I wouldn't remember the Mistress of the Whitewood?"

"Then it must be Lady Aubrey."

"How in the name of the Elder Races did you guess that?"

"She's the only other mage of Merceria who's a woman."

The vard shook his head. "I must admit you've changed since you spent all that time amongst them."

"For the better, I hope?"

"That remains to be seen."

The next morning, Kasri made her way through the halls of Ironcliff. Though technically a city, the vast majority of it tunnelled into the side of a mountain, leading to corridors instead of streets, but to one of the mountain folk, it was all one and the same.

She slowed as she neared the doors to Agramath's study. Outside stood a member of the Hearth Guard, her own company of elite warriors, but all he did at her approach was nod in recognition.

"Is Lord Agramath within?" she asked.

"He is, Commander," replied the guard. "Along with the Human spellcaster. Shall I announce you?"

"If you would be so kind. Please ask him if he's available to speak with me at this time."

The guard cracked open the door and slipped inside. Moments later, he opened it fully, allowing her passage.

"Kasri," called out a voice. "So nice to see you again."

"Lady Aubrey, you grace us with your presence. I assume nothing is amiss in Wincaster?"

"Not at all. Master Bloom brought me to Ironcliff to commit the magic circle to memory. I was just making the necessary arrangements with Master Agramath."

"To which I have readily agreed," added the master of rock and stone.

"And Master Revi Bloom?"

"He left earlier this morning," said Aubrey.

"But you didn't come here to talk to her," said Agramath.

"How did you know?" replied Kasri.

"The surprise on your face."

"You have me there. I'll admit I knew she was in Ironcliff, but I didn't know she'd be here with you at this particular moment."

"If there's a problem," said Aubrey, "I can give you some privacy?"

"No, it's rather fortuitous you're here. I've got a little favour to ask."

"Which is?"

"I need to go to Wincaster."

"Need?" said Agramath. "Or want?"

"A little of both, I suppose."

"I should be happy to take you there," said Aubrey, "once I complete studying the circle."

"And how long will that take?"

"That depends on when I can start." Aubrey looked at Agramath.

"Right away, if you like," said the Dwarven mage.

"In that case, I'll be ready to leave by noon. Will that suit you?"

"It will, indeed."

"Might I ask the reason for the visit? I'm certain the queen would like to be informed if you're coming on official business."

"It's not official, just personal."

"Really?" said Agramath, eyeing her suspiciously. "What's that mean?"

"It's none of your business."

He blustered a bit before turning and moving things around on his workbench.

Kasri, meanwhile, turned her full attention to Lady Aubrey. "I might be a little late. I have an audience with my father, the vard."

"I'm in no hurry. If you're late, I'll wait for you."

"That would be much appreciated, thank you. I'll come to find you once I'm ready to depart."

"Might I invite you to dine with us this evening?"

"Us?"

"Yes, at Lord Richard's Wincaster estate. Beverly and Aldwin will be there."

"I'm afraid I'll be visiting a friend."

"Bring him along too."

Agramath's ears pricked up. "What's this, now? Who's this 'him' you're referring to?"

Kasri frowned. "Again, none of your business."

"I'm only trying to look out for you. You are, after all, the named successor to the vard."

"Yes, something no one will ever let me forget." She looked at Aubrey. "My apologies. You shouldn't have to listen to all of this bickering."

"That's quite all right. I quite miss it, actually."

"You miss bickering?"

"Yes. I used to have two brothers. They died in the war."

"Killed by the Norlanders?"

"No," said Aubrey. "By the king's men during the civil war."

Agramath paled. "Civil war! Are you saying they fought against their rightful king? Perhaps we were a little premature allying ourselves with these Mercerians?"

"Nonsense," said Kasri. "The war brought Queen Anna to the Throne, which has only aided our cause. Now, why don't you get back to whatever you were doing with all that stuff on your table, and allow us to deal with politics." She winked at Aubrey before lowering her voice. "He loves a good argument every now and again."

"It's time I visit that magic circle," said the Mercerian noble. "It won't commit itself to memory."

"I'll show you the way. After all, someone has to inform the guards you've been granted access."

· · ·

Leaving Aubrey at the magic circle, Kasri continued to the Royal Chambers, where she waited while her father consulted with yet another guild member, this time from the potters guild, if the guard was to be believed.

The door finally opened, revealing a Dwarf, bent with age, sporting a snowy-white beard hanging almost to the floor. The vard waited until the fellow shuffled off down the hallway before turning to his daughter.

"Come in, Kasri. Let us talk more of your Mercerian adventures." He led her inside, then moved closer to the fireplace, warming his hands. "Now, what did you want to speak to me about?"

"I was thinking about what you said."

"You'll need to refresh my memory. What, in particular, are you referring to?"

"That I need to forge. I've decided that's what I'm going to do. At least I'm going to attempt it."

Her father's gaze snapped up from the fire to her. "Attempt? Are you suggesting he might actually refuse you?"

"It's a distinct possibility, yes."

He laughed but cut it short when she frowned. "Sorry. I didn't mean to offend. Tell me, is it someone I know?"

"No. The truth is, he's not from Ironcliff."

"Not from Ironcliff, you say? How intriguing. Is he a guild master, by chance?"

"No, but he is a master smith."

"That's excellent news. What is his standing in the guild?"

"That's what I wanted to talk to you about."

"I'm not sure I understand?"

"He's not a member of a guild."

Her father stared back, his face blank. "I'm sorry? He is at least a Dwarf, I hope?"

"He is. Herdwin by name."

"And you say he's a master smith?"

"That's what I said, yes. He crafted a sword for the Queen of Merceria and helped build the forge that created Nature's Fury."

"Nature's Fury?" said Thalgrun. "Wasn't that Dame Beverly's weapon? The one made from sky metal?"

"Indeed."

"Yet you say he doesn't belong to a guild. How can that be?"

"That is not my story to tell. Suffice it to say they had a parting of the ways some years ago."

Thalgrun shook his head. "Of all those you had to choose from, why this guildless smith?"

"It was never my intent, but we became close during the war to liberate Weldwyn."

"Then stay friends and forge with another. That would be a better solution."

"But I don't want to forge with another."

"You are to be vard one day, Kasri. How do you expect the guilds to take you seriously when your own forge mate refuses membership?"

"Surely it's better he does not? That way, he can claim no favourites?"

The vard frowned. "You know as well as I how powerful the guilds are, here in Ironcliff."

"More powerful than even the vard?"

"I hate to admit it, but yes."

"Is there no other solution?"

"Talk to him, convince him to rejoin the guild. Perhaps he could win some influence in fifty years or so?"

"I don't want to wait fifty years to forge!"

"Is he aware of your intentions?"

She blushed. "Not yet. I only just realized it myself."

"Why is that?"

"I suppose my return to Ironcliff made me realize how much I'd come to appreciate his companionship." She forced a laugh. "You may get your wish, after all, if he rejects me."

"Rejects you? What nonsense is this? In the name of Gundar, why would he reject you?"

"For the very reasons you mention. I fear he may see himself as unworthy, despite his heroics."

"Heroics?"

"Yes. He's an accomplished warrior and an experienced leader in battle."

"This is a difficult situation, to be sure," said the vard. "But perhaps all is not lost."

"Meaning?"

"If he is guildless as you say—"

"He is!"

Shocked by her outburst, Thalgrun paused momentarily. "As I was saying, it's not unreasonable to assume an arrangement could be made with whatever guild he had differences with. Was it the smiths guild of Stonecastle?"

"It was."

"Would he be willing to travel there and settle the matter once and for all?"

"And if he did, that would allow us to forge?"

"It is not the forging that's the problem," said Thalgrun. "It's your position as successor to the Crown of Ironcliff."

"And if the matter remains unresolved?"

"Then it may well come down to choosing between forging or one-day becoming vard." He moved closer, taking her hands in his. "I only want what's best for you, Kas, but I can't upend centuries of tradition to go against the guilds—it would be suicidal. Surely you can understand that?"

"I can," said Kasri. "Though it gives me no pleasure to do so."

"So, you'll talk to this fellow? What's his name again?"

"Herdwin, Herdwin Steelarm. And yes, I'll speak to him, but I don't know if he'll heed your advice."

"I assume he's in Wincaster?"

"He is."

"When will you leave?"

"Today. Lady Aubrey offered to take me there, using magic."

Thalgrun shuddered. "This whole recall spell puts me on edge. Why can't you march there like any normal Dwarf?"

She laughed. "That would take weeks, and besides, Lady Aubrey invited me to dinner with her cousin."

"Her cousin? Who's that?"

"Dame Beverly."

"I had no idea they were related. It seems you travelled in august company."

"So did you, remember?"

"Yes… well, that's only to be expected. I am the vard after all."

"Naturally, I shall return Stormhammer before I go."

"Why would you do that?"

"Your father gave it to you."

"Yes," said the vard. "Just as I gave it to you. Stormhammer is yours to wield now, Kas, whether or not you rule as vard."

"You honour me."

"No, it is you who honours me. Will you take your armour?"

"I didn't intend to. After all, I'm not going to Wincaster to fight."

"Still, you might bring a shirt of Dwarven mail, just to be on the safe side."

"Very well, I shall take my old training armour. Will that suffice?"

"And a full helm, of course. You can't go advertising the fact you're female."

"For Gundar's sake, Father. I'm going to Wincaster, not the frontier."

"Still, you never know where life might take you, and I insist."

"Very well."

"Oh, and Kasri?"

"Yes, Father?"

"I love you."

"And I, you, but sometimes you can be a little pushy."

Thalgrun laughed. "That's one of the perks of being vard!"

TWO

Wincaster

AUTUMN 966 MC

Land of swordsmen, axe, and bow,
Merceria, kingdom proud.
And therein lies the master smith,
His Dwarven anvil loud.

Herdwin Steelarm was his name,
His exploits legendary.
But he, amongst his many deeds,
Ne'er did find time to marry.

Herdwin lifted the blade from the quenching oil, holding it aloft to examine its quality. Satisfied with the result, he set it aside before taking off his gloves, and wiped his brow.

His sweat flowed freely as the forge's heat filled his

workshop, so he made his way to the door and opened it wide, letting the afternoon breeze cool him. His face lit up when he noticed a familiar figure coming down the street.

"Kasri, is that you? What in the name of the Gods are you doing here in Wincaster?"

"I came to see you," she replied, her face breaking into a grin. "I hope I didn't come at a bad time?"

"Not at all. I was just taking a break."

"Working on armour?"

"No, a sword."

"A commission?"

"Yes, for Beverly. A gift for her husband."

"And is it complete?"

"Not yet, but at least I'm done with the blade. There's still some work left on the handle, though." He noted her awkward stance. She appeared to be waiting for something. "Pardon my manners," he said. "Won't you come in?"

"I'd be delighted." Kasri stepped into the workshop, her gaze roaming the space.

"Are you here on a diplomatic mission? Something on behalf of your father, perhaps?"

"No. As I said, I'm here to see you."

"You came all the way to Wincaster just to see me?"

"I did. Does that surprise you?"

"Only in a good way."

"The truth is, I returned to Ironcliff only to discover how much I missed your company."

"I feel the same."

Kasri's smile warmed his heart.

"Are you hungry?" he asked.

"Not especially, but there's something I wanted to talk to you about."

"Very well. What is it?"

"I'm considering forging," said Kasri.

Herdwin's legs grew weak, and he sat down on a nearby stool to hide his discomfort. "Forging?" he said, his mouth suddenly dry. "To whom?"

"You."

His heart began racing. "Me? But I'm nothing but a smith and not even a guild member at that."

"I don't care. Well, let me clarify that. I do care, but not in the way you might think."

"I'm afraid you have me at a loss."

She walked over to the small cot nearby. "May I?"

"By all means."

She sat, trying to compose her thoughts. "I've given this matter considerable attention since we parted."

"I can imagine." He let out a breath. "Sorry. I didn't mean to interrupt. Please continue."

"As you are aware, it's entirely within my rights to choose whom to forge with, regardless of their guild status. If that were the only thing I needed to worry about, I'd have no concerns, but the fact of the matter is I'm the vard's designated successor, and as such, any potential forge mate…" Her voice choked up.

"Must belong to a guild?" he asked.

She merely nodded, adding to her forlorn countenance.

"Were it within my power," continued Herdwin, "I would become a guild master, but you and I both know that's not how this works."

"But you were an apprentice once. Does that not still make you a member?"

"It might, were it not for my leaving Stonecastle. There's also the fact I passed on knowledge to non-guild members, and Human ones at that."

"You're talking about Aldwin Fitzwilliam?"

"I am, and I doubt it will win me any favours."

Kasri took a breath. "Can you please explain the exact nature of your relationship with the smiths guild?"

"You mean why I'm here in Wincaster instead of Stonecastle?"

"Yes. It can't be your skill; I've seen your work, and the Vard of Stonecastle gave you command of his warriors, which speaks volumes. Why, then, does the guild hate you so when its vard holds you in such high regard?"

"It's a long story, best told over a tankard of ale."

Kasri stood. "You had me at ale. Where do we find it in these parts?"

"Give me a moment to clean myself up, and I'll take you to the Queen's Arms."

"Is that a tavern?"

"Not just any tavern," said Herdwin, "but one of the best in town. It's near the Palace."

"Is that far?"

"No, not at all."

"I imagine it's expensive. Are you sure you can afford it?"

"Why? Don't you think you're worth it?"

She blushed, and he smiled.

"Come now," he continued. "Let me wash up, and we'll be on our way."

. . .

The Queen's Arms was a busy place, but at the sight of Herdwin, a serving girl quickly ushered them to a seat.

"Clearly, you're a regular," said Kasri.

"Yes. I often come here for a tankard or two."

"Oh? And who do you drink with?"

"An old friend of mine, if you must know."

She leaned on the table, glaring at him. "I see, and what's her name?"

"Gerald," he replied with a smirk. "You know, the marshal?"

"You drink with the marshal?"

"Of course. I've known him for years. I used to repair weapons for his men when he was only a sergeant."

"Is that how you met the queen?"

"It was, though, at the time he introduced her as his daughter."

"You're certainly at home amongst these Humans," said Kasri. "Was it hard to adjust when you first came to Wincaster?"

"A little, but I soon got used to it."

"And what was the hardest thing to accept?"

He sat there for a moment as a server brought two tankards of ale.

Kasri looked up at her in surprise. "How did you know what to bring?"

"Easy," the woman replied. "Master Herdwin here always orders the same thing."

"And me?"

"I've yet to see one of your race who doesn't like ale. If you want, I can switch for something else?"

"No," said Kasri. "Ale will be fine. Thank you."

The girl made her way back through the busy tavern while Herdwin continued mulling things over.

"So?" she prompted. "You were going to tell me the hardest thing to accept when you first arrived?"

"Yes. That's right, I was. My apologies."

"Well, what was it?"

"How they treat their females. In our society, we hold them in great respect, and, if I'm being honest, some here do the same, but by and large, most are treated abysmally."

"Why do you think that is?"

"I don't know," said Herdwin. "Perhaps it's because they're more numerous? Or that their society is run mostly by men."

"Yet they have a queen."

"They do, but that's a more recent development, and you and I both know how entrenched beliefs can get."

Kasri took a sip of her ale. "You're referring to our system of guilds."

"I am."

"Which brings us back to your situation."

"I see I'm not going to be able to avoid the subject."

"Is it something that upsets you?" she asked.

His face fell. "Only in that it makes it impossible for us to forge."

"Why would you say that?"

He lifted his eyes to meet hers. "It wouldn't be right for a vard to forge with someone who's guildless."

"But you led the Dwarves of Stonecastle in battle, and you're a close ally, an advisor even, to the Queen of Merceria."

"Neither of which holds any weight back home."

"Maybe it would help if you told me about your issues with the guild."

"Like most of our people, I came of age and began my apprenticeship in different trades."

"As we all do. I apprenticed to a potters guild before I found my true calling as a warrior."

"And I, a carpenter before becoming a smith. Now, I don't know about the warriors guild, but a smith remains an apprentice for many years before being elevated to full membership. I learned my trade, and I daresay I became very good, completing everything I needed to receive full membership."

"I sense a but," said Kasri.

"Then your instincts are correct. Advancement in the smiths guild in Stonecastle is by seniority. They keep a tight grip on how many can be members at any one time."

"So, you were stuck?"

"That's about the size of it. I hung on for decades, but until you're a full member, you're not allowed to sell your own wares. Essentially, you're making free goods for the guild's profits."

"They paid you nothing?"

"Well, almost nothing. Room, board, and a modest stipend, which would only purchase the cheapest ales."

"And that's when you left?"

"No, it's a little more complicated than that. I began

delving into matters my mentor felt only fitting for a master smith. I might've even supplemented my income by selling off some of my work, all in contravention of guild rules."

"What happened?"

"They brought me before the guild master, who stripped me of my seniority and placed me back at the bottom of the list. It would've taken at least another half a century for me to gain full membership. That's when I decided I'd had enough."

"So, you fled to Wincaster?"

"Yes. Thankfully, my cousins raised sufficient funds to get me started here, else I would've starved. I've been busy ever since."

"And this guild master, is he still in charge?"

"Yes. Well, at least he was the last I heard. He's an obstinate fellow by the name of Grennik Ironbeard."

"I gather he's old?"

"Ancient," said Herdwin. "Not that his age matters so much as his stubbornness."

"I can understand your hesitancy to settle this."

Herdwin reached across the table, taking her hand. "How important is this to you?"

"Very. My father made it clear that if I am to forge, it must be with a guild member."

"Then I shall go to Stonecastle and settle matters."

"You would be willing to do that for me?"

"Yes. Does that surprise you?"

"Surprise me, no. It makes me very happy. Might I ask that you allow me to accompany you to Stonecastle?"

"Don't you trust me?"

"Of course I do, but I want to be there to support you. That's what friends do, and I consider you one of my closest friends."

He smiled. "Yes, I gathered that from the fact you want to forge with me."

"So it's settled, then," said Kasri. "We'll travel to Stonecastle together, though I've little idea where it is."

"Leave that to me," said Herdwin. "I've made the trip more times than I care to admit."

"You've gone back?"

"Of course. I still have family there, and the guilds ignore me as long as I'm only visiting. I'd be interested to see how they react to your presence, though."

"It's probably best if I didn't advertise my position. It might put them off."

"I think it would have precisely the opposite effect, but the choice is yours."

"When should we leave?"

"Let me think on that," said Herdwin, rubbing his chin. "There's that commission to finish, but that shouldn't be more than a day or two. I'll bake some stonecakes while I'm at it. We'll need them on the trip. Shall we say the end of the week?"

"Sounds good to me."

"Excellent. I'll see you then."

Kasri grinned. "You're not getting out of things that easily."

"Whatever do you mean?"

"We're invited to dine with Lady Aubrey at her uncle's. Dame Beverly will be there, along with Aldwin, of course."

"Wonderful. I can catch up on his attempts to produce plate armour."

"You know the place?"

"I do."

"Then I'll see you there tonight."

"Tonight?"

"Disappointed?"

He grinned. "Not at all. In fact, I'm looking forward to it."

Kasri downed the rest of her ale and then stood. "Good. Now I must be off."

"So soon?"

"We'll have plenty of time to chat later. There's a city to explore. I'd invite you to join me, but you have work to do."

"So I do," said Herdwin. He stood, his ale unfinished. "It's good to see you, Kasri."

"And you."

"So," said Lord Richard, "I hear you're both going to Stonecastle?"

"News travels fast," said Herdwin.

"I told him," said Kasri. "I felt it only proper as he offered me a room here while we wait."

"And quite rightly, too," said Albreda. "Tell me, Kasri. Have you ever visited Stonecastle?"

"No. Ironcliff is the only Dwarven stronghold I know. Why, have you been there?"

"No. I prefer a more woodsy environment."

"You might like the Darkwood," suggested Herdwin.

"Are there a lot of animals there?" asked Albreda.

"I haven't a clue. I've stuck to the roads on all my trips through the forest. Still, I would expect they must farm some animals, or else how would they eat?"

"What do they eat in Stonecastle?" asked Aubrey. "I don't imagine there are many farm animals up in the mountains."

"You'd be right," said Herdwin, "although we have a lot of goats and sheep. Of course, they don't live inside the mount. That would be ridiculous."

"The mount?"

"The name we give to the part of the city within the mountain itself."

"And how much is that compared to the outer portion?"

"Oh, I don't know, perhaps two-thirds?"

Beverly looked at Herdwin's plate with a grin. "That said, it appears you and Kasri both have a taste for meat."

"Aye, when we can get it."

"Ironcliff has plenty of farms outside," added Kasri, "though we don't eat meat for every meal."

"Then what do you eat instead?" asked Beverly.

"Lots of things," replied the Dwarven smith. "My favourite was probably mushrooms, though potatoes are nice too."

"Yes," added Kasri. "Especially with a blue fungus topping."

"I don't know about you," said Aldwin, "but that sounds about as far from tasty as I can imagine."

"Nonsense, it's delicious. Of course, you Humans don't have the same sense of taste as us, so you might find it as unpalatable as you suggest. Still, you should at least try it before you criticize it."

"So, when are you off to Stonecastle?" asked Lord Richard.

"The end of the week," said Herdwin. "There's some work to finish up first."

"Will you be heading through the Darkwood?"

"Of course. It's the fastest route."

"And will you travel by horse?" asked Aubrey.

"No, by foot. Horses would only slow us down in the mountains, not to mention the lack of fodder for them in Stonecastle."

"Might I offer an alternative?" asked Albreda. "I'm sure Beverly could arrange a carriage to take you to the Darkwood?"

"That would shorten the trip," said Herdwin, "but I don't want to be a bother."

"It's no bother," said Beverly. "We regularly send dispatches to the Darkwood. It's simple enough to add a carriage. They can drop you at the Last Hope Inn, along with our correspondence. You'd be doing us a favour, as long as you don't mind meeting some Elves."

"That's a marvellous idea," said Kasri. "I didn't spend much time with them during the war."

"That's because they're notoriously solitary," said Herdwin, "tending to only socialize with their own kind."

"Yes," agreed Beverly. "That's been my experience as well. Still, we've made good progress of late in that regard."

"You have?"

"Yes. Aubrey is working with them to solve their problem."

"And what problem is that?" asked Kasri.

"They cannot bear children," replied the Life Mage. "It's an issue that's been around for centuries. I won't go into details, but Kraloch and I believe we might have found a solution."

"Kraloch?"

"Yes, the Orc shaman? Surely you met him during the war?"

"I think so, but I must confess it's hard to keep track of all the names."

"Understandable," offered Lord Richard. "I have the same problem trying to remember all the new nobles of Merceria. Yourself excluded, Lord Herdwin."

Kasri let her gaze drift towards her fellow Dwarf. "Lord Herdwin?"

"Yes," continued the baron. "Didn't he tell you? He represents Stonecastle on the Nobles Council. He's the equivalent of an earl; technically, he outranks me."

"That's only an honorary title," said Herdwin, his face reddening.

"Still, it puts him in great standing in Merceria. Of course, he's not the heir to the Crown like you are, Lady Kasri. It is Lady Kasri we use to identify you, isn't it?"

"No, just Kasri, and I'm not an heir. Dwarven rule isn't determined by blood but by choice of the reigning vard. That would be king or queen to you Humans."

"Then what is your title?"

"Successor," offered Herdwin, "at least for now."

"Whatever does that mean?" asked Beverly.

"It means," explained Kasri, "that it's the ruler's prerogative to announce a new successor at any time."

"And is that common?"

"Common enough. A vard usually picks someone they feel will carry on with their wishes after death. One with the same vision, if you will."

"And in the case of Ironcliff," said Albreda, "that's you, at present?"

"It is, but my father likely has quite a few years left in him, plenty of time for him to change his mind."

"And he lets you do whatever you want in the meantime?"

Kasri grinned. "I'd like to see him try to stop me!"

THREE

The Last Hope

AUTUMN 966 MC

When these two Dwarves did meet at last,
They found their hearts entwined.
And though from different lands, it seemed,
They were of likened mind.

So, to the east, the duo went,
Their noble quest begun.
For the marriage of these heroes two,
Was something to be won.

T he carriage hit a bump, sending Kasri scrambling to stay in her seat. Herdwin chuckled.

"You think that's funny?" asked Kasri.

"Not at all, but I well remember the first time I sat in one of these things. It turned out much as it has for you."

"Then what's the secret to remaining in place?"

"Push yourself all the way to the back of your seat and rest your arm on the window. You'll still bounce around, but at least you won't fall."

She stood up, a difficult act with the way they were jostling around, then sat down again, but not across from him as Herdwin expected. Instead, she squeezed in beside him.

"There," she said. "Now we'll keep each other in place." She held the window frame to her left with an iron grip.

Herdwin gazed out the window to hide his amusement. Sergeant Gardner and his men rode on either side, looking for bandits who might trouble them. However, it was unlikely, for this part of the countryside was one of the safest in the kingdom. Then again, one could never be entirely sure, and he felt thankful for their escort's presence.

"How much farther?" asked Kasri.

"Not long, now. Once we get over this hill, you'll be able to see the Darkwood in the distance. It's well named, I can tell you."

"Are the trees black?"

"No, but their boughs are a very dark green, more so than you might expect."

"I've seen few forests in my time, so I'm not expecting much of anything."

"Then you won't be disappointed. On the forest's western end is the Last Hope Inn, run by a fellow by the name of Falcon."

"Like the bird?"

"Precisely. He owns the place, though I must warn you it's not the most glamorous of inns."

"Why? What's wrong with it?"

"He's notoriously cheap, at least he used to be. The food was barely tolerable, but I admit I haven't passed this way for some time."

Kasri shrugged. "It makes little difference to me; there are plenty of stonecakes."

"At least we'll have a bed for the night." He suddenly realized what he'd said and turned away in embarrassment. "I mean, we'll both have a bed... that is, we'll EACH have a bed."

She laughed. "I understand what you meant. No insult was taken. What's this Falcon fellow like?"

"He doesn't speak much, but he's in contact with the Elves."

"How did he arrange that?"

"He used to be a King's Ranger."

"Which is?"

"The rangers keep peace on the kingdom's roads."

"Aren't they a part of the army?"

"They are in times of war. The rest of the time, they enforce the laws of the land."

"And so he retired and built this inn? What's it called again?"

"The Last Hope."

"Not exactly the most inspiring of names," she replied.

"We need only stay long enough to get permission to enter the Darkwood."

"And how long will that take?"

"Likely no more than a day. In the meantime, we'll have a roof over our heads."

"And a warm fire, I hope. The weather is growing considerably cooler of late. Back in Ironcliff, we'd be getting ready for winter by now."

"Not so in Merceria; this is harvest season. Mind you, they will long since have pulled in the crops where we're going."

"Is that because of the weather?"

"Indeed. Stonecastle is a frigid place, much more so than Ironcliff, from what you've described. Of course, the greater portion of the population lives under the mountain, but my cousin's house is in the outer city, so I'm afraid we'll need to manage as best we can."

"That's all right. I brought a warm cloak."

A cry from outside drew their attention. Herdwin leaned out the window. "Something wrong, Sergeant?"

"The Last Hope is in sight, my lord. We shall be there shortly."

"Thank you." He sat back down. "It appears we are almost at our first stop."

Kasri looked out at the distant structure but said nothing. Soon, the carriage slowed.

"I shall miss riding in this contraption," she said. "It's a pity we don't have these back home."

"I doubt it would be much use in the mountains."

"Perhaps," she replied, "but a lot of Ironcliff lies outside the walls."

"And where would you place such a conveyance should war come?"

"I'd hardly concern myself with its safety if Ironcliff was under attack." She glanced around the confines. "Then again, I daresay a few arbalesters could be put in here, not to mention on the carriage roof. Perhaps it could be adapted to a war machine?"

"An interesting observance," said Herdwin, "but I fear such thoughts should wait, for we must gather our things."

Once the carriage came to a stop, Herdwin opened the door. The ground appeared an impossible distance away, but then one of their escorts produced a small step, enabling them to descend.

"You can both go inside," said Sergeant Gardner. "I'll see your packs safely delivered."

"And the dispatches," said Herdwin. "Don't forget those. I'll see that they are safely delivered."

"Of course, and thank you again, my lord, for doing this on behalf of the Crown."

"My pleasure." He held out his hand to Kasri. "Shall we?"

They entered the Last Hope. As far as inns go, it was a modest affair, boasting only two rooms on the ground floor, while the common area consisted of three tables and a fireplace. Out from the back room came an Elven server.

"This is new," said Herdwin.

"Greetings. I am Elariel. Welcome to the Last Hope. Will you require rooms?"

"That depends. Do you have any available?"

"We do. Two, in fact."

"Then we'll take them both."

"Would you like something to eat?"

"That would be marvellous, thank you. Before you go, might you answer a question?"

"If I can."

"Where's Falcon?"

"Away on business. I have authority to act on his behalf."

"Does that include the food?"

"As long as you don't mind Elvish fare."

"Which is?" asked Kasri.

"Lots of vegetables," answered Herdwin. "But they mix in small amounts of meat. It's at least tolerable."

"If you take a seat, I shall fetch you some food," said Elariel. "And something to drink?"

"How about some ale?" asked Kasri.

"No," said Herdwin. "Anything but that. How about some nice Elvish wine?"

Elariel nodded, then headed off to the kitchen.

"What's wrong with the ale?"

"Unfortunately, I've had it before. Trust me. You don't want to drink that stuff."

Kasri stared back in wonder. "How does someone mess up ale?"

"I have no idea, but they found a way. Have you ever tried Elvish wine?"

"Only the stuff they served amongst the Mercerians. I understand the queen has a liking for it."

"She does, not that she drinks much."

"Are you suggesting she doesn't drink alcohol?"

"Only in moderation," said Herdwin. "Beverly's the same."

"Yes, I noticed that. Why do you think that is?"

"Humans can't handle it like us mountain folk."

"So, what's the plan for tomorrow?"

Herdwin paused as a Mercerian warrior deposited their packs near the entrance, then departed. "Assuming we get the all-clear, we'll head into the Darkwood."

"And how do we find Lord Greycloak?"

"We don't—he finds us. You can't go two steps into the Darkwood without the Forest Wardens watching you. That's why we must wait to enter—so that they can get into place. Of course, you'd never know they were there."

"We're to be watched the entire time? Not exactly the most trusting of people, are they?"

"There aren't any Elves up near Ironcliff?"

"There are," she replied, "but they're Wood Elves, much smaller in stature, and from what I'm aware of, they live quite differently than the Elves of the Darkwood."

"Different, how?"

"Their communities are smaller, their buildings more like the Orcs. Not that there's anything wrong with that, of course."

"Well, the Elves here are nothing like that."

"I know. I saw them during the war. What's an Elf city look like?"

"I wouldn't know. I've never seen it."

"How many times have you gone through the Darkwood?"

"Oh, let me think on that. A dozen, at least, over the last fifty years."

"And you never laid eyes on their city?"

"No," said Herdwin. "It's a closely guarded secret." He

leaned across the table, lowering his voice. "You know, there's a rumour they don't even have cities, that the entire thing is one big lie meant to impress the rest of us."

"What are you suggesting they live in, trees?"

He shrugged. "I've heard worse."

"They must have cities."

"What makes you say that?"

"They produce weapons and armour. That alone requires smiths, and I very much doubt you could build a smithy up in the trees."

"All right," said Herdwin. "I'll give you that, but we still have no idea what they look like."

"Has anyone ever asked?"

"Asked?"

"Yes," said Kasri. "Perhaps they're waiting for someone to ask for an invitation?"

"I… never thought of that. I suppose you might be right." He smiled. "I can see you're much more than a pretty face."

"Oh? I don't believe anyone's ever said that I'm pretty before."

"Really?"

She laughed. "Of course I have. I'm a female Dwarf, but it's nice to hear it from one who truly means it."

Herdwin was still blushing when Elariel returned with two bowls of food.

"This smells delicious," said Kasri. "Thank you."

"You're welcome," replied the Elf. "Now, I shall fetch your wine. I assume you're here to gain entry to the Darkwood?"

"We are."

"Then I will send word on your behalf."

"Might you give us some indication of when we can expect a reply?"

"Likely not until morning," said Elariel, "but if we hear anything before then, I will be sure to let you know." Once more, she disappeared into the kitchen.

"Well," said Herdwin. "This is nicer than what was here the last time."

"Which was?"

"Some sort of sausage, though I'm not sure what kind of meat they used. Gerald once told me they were the worst sausages he ever ate."

"But he still ate them?"

"Oh yes. The Marshal of Merceria is not one to pass up a sausage, no matter how bad it may taste."

"You seem to know him well."

"I count him amongst my closest friends."

Kasri used her spoon to sample the food. "It's as good as it smells."

They fell silent as they ate, speaking only to acknowledge the wine their host brought. Kasri was the first one done, setting down her spoon and waiting until Herdwin finished.

"What are your cousins like?" she asked. "Will we be staying with your parents?"

"No. My mother passed some time ago."

"And your father?"

"Died in a rockfall, just like my Great Uncle Bremel. They were both miners."

"A pity they didn't have a master of rock and stone. They can do much to prevent such things."

"Unfortunately, Stonecastle is no longer blessed when it comes to mages. I hear you've got one back in Ironcliff, though."

"We do: Master Agramath."

"And are there others?"

"A few, but none as powerful as he, and certainly not as many as the Mercerians. Mages, I mean, not just masters of rock and stone."

"Yes," he agreed, "and thank the Gods for their healers. Our losses would've been horrendous if it weren't for people like Lady Aubrey."

"And the rest of your family?"

"We'll stay with my cousin Gelion and his wife."

"And her name is?"

"Margel. She's a member of the stonemasons guild."

"And Gelion?"

"Warriors guild, much like yourself, although admittedly, without the benefit of your status as successor. He captains one of Stonecastle's companies."

"How interesting. Foot or bow?"

"Arbalesters," he replied. "His warriors can often be found manning the watchtowers we use to keep an eye on the area. You'll see one once we get into the mountains."

"How many of these towers are there?"

"I'm not entirely sure. There's one on the road, a few farther to the east, with the rest scattered throughout the mountains surrounding Stonecastle. They're designed to give us advanced warning should an attack come. Mind you, the beacons haven't been lit for hundreds of years. Except for midwinter, that's when we test them."

"You miss it, don't you?"

"What makes you say that?" he asked.

"You said 'we' instead of 'they'."

"Parts of it I miss, especially family."

"It must be hard living alone with no relatives nearby."

"It is, but it's the life I chose."

"Once we're forged, will we remain in Wincaster or live in Ironcliff?"

"You mean IF we forge. I still harbour doubts the guild will take me back."

"Very well, I'll play your game. Let's assume everything works out in our favour. What then?"

"That's a very interesting thing to consider."

"Remember," said Kasri, "we can now use magic to transfer from Wincaster to Ironcliff. Nothing says we have to settle in only one place."

"True, but one day you'll be vard. Surely, you're not suggesting you could get away with living in Wincaster?"

"Let's not worry about that. It's not something I want to consider."

"You brought it up."

"I know. I just didn't think it would bother me so much."

He reached across, placing his hand on hers. "I would be happy to live anywhere if you were there."

"Thank you," she said. "That means a lot to me, but I'm not sure I could ask you to give up your livelihood."

"I could always work a forge up in Ironcliff."

"Not without the sanction of the smiths guild."

"All the more reason for me to settle things in Stonecastle." He tasted his wine. "Say, that's not bad. Not as good as Dwarven ale, but I could get used to it."

"Maybe you should buy some bottles."

"For what?"

"A gift for Gelion and Margel."

"That's not a bad idea. I think I shall. Do you want to take any to Ironcliff?"

"If I did, I'd wait until we're on the way home. I don't want to lug a bottle to Stonecastle only to bring it back here."

"That's a fair point."

The sunlight outside died off, leaving only the fire's glow illuminating the room. Elariel appeared, lighting candles throughout, despite only two guests.

"Your rooms are ready when you are," she announced.

"Then I should take up our packs," said Herdwin.

"Already taken care of, Master Herdwin."

He stared back. "How did you know my name?"

"Your reputation precedes you, Master Dwarf."

"I'm not sure I follow?"

"I served with Lord Arandil at the siege of Summersgate. I saw you storm the city wall, a brave attack against perilous odds."

"And my companion?"

"She is also known to me, for who can forget the great dragon rider? It is an honour for both of you to stay here at the Last Hope. Now, shall I show you to your rooms, or do you wish to linger here a while longer?"

"We should go to bed," suggested Kasri. "It's likely to be a busy day tomorrow, assuming they grant us passage."

"Very well," said the Elf. "I will turn down your blankets." She climbed the stairs, disappearing from sight.

"What do you make of that?" asked Herdwin. "Turn down the blankets? What are they doing, making demands that can't be met?"

"It is a strange turn of phrase, to be sure, but I doubt it means what you think."

Herdwin shrugged. "Perhaps not, but we'll never know if we don't go and look."

Herdwin woke up to a face staring down at him.

"Kasri? Is something wrong?"

"Not at all, but it's time you got up. Breakfast is ready, and there's news."

"You mean—"

"Yes, they granted us permission to enter the Darkwood, but Elariel said we must hurry, for there's a long walk ahead of us."

He made to rise, but then remembered he wasn't wearing anything. "I'll meet you downstairs once I'm decent."

She grinned. "Are you suggesting you're not fully clothed under those blankets?"

His crimson cheeks gave her the answer she sought. "Very well, I shall await your presence downstairs."

He waited until the door closed before leaping out of bed. He quickly threw on his clothes, then barrelled down into the common room, where Kasri sat at a table, staring at a plate containing some sort of bread with a small pat of butter and golden liquid covering it.

"Is that syrup?" he asked.

"So I'm told, but I've never seen this before, have you?"

"Can't say I have. What is it?"

"Elariel called it a flatcake. Apparently, it's a common meal for Elves." She sliced off a piece with her knife, then speared it, shovelling it into her mouth.

"Well? How is it?"

"Delicious. Come try some." She cut off another piece and held it up to him. He bit it, but the syrup dripped down his beard. "Mmm," he mumbled. "Very nice. I wonder how it would travel."

"Fine, I would imagine, as long as you don't put syrup on them beforehand, although they would be cold."

"Let's find out, shall we? We'll ask Elariel for some to take with us."

FOUR

The Darkwood

AUTUMN 966 MC

Into the forest, they would go,
In darkened wood confined.
And there within the many boughs,
An Elven bard did find.

He wrote the song I sing to you,
Of journey with these two.
And as for story, take my word,
I tell you all is true.

The road into the Darkwood was little more than a woodland trail, meandering through thick trunks of giant trees. Soon, it grew broader and straighter, and by noon, the boughs that kept them in perpetual gloom began thinning out, allowing the sun to reveal itself, bathing the entire area in a golden hue, lifting their spirits, and increasing their pace.

"I never would've imagined seeing such a thing," said Kasri. "It's beautiful."

"Aye, it is, isn't it? I would've told you about it earlier, but I felt it best to let you see for yourself."

"Is it always this bright?"

"Yes," said Herdwin, "though the autumn colours accentuate the effect. We are now in what I like to call the heart of the forest, but it goes on for many miles."

"How many miles?"

"Sixty or seventy, by my reckoning, but it's hard to estimate with no landmarks."

"Several days of walking, then."

"Yes, but there are clearings along the way. However, I must warn you not to leave the trail."

"Not even for a call of nature?"

"That shouldn't be a problem, but never go out of sight of the road, or you may be lost forever. They say the Darkwood can swallow a person, never to be seen again."

"But we're being watched, aren't we?"

"We are," he replied, "but to leave the trail is a death sentence."

"Come now. Are you seriously suggesting they would kill a traveller just for walking in the woods?"

"It's been so for as long as I've lived. The Elves are a secretive people who guard their homes against all intruders."

"Then perhaps it's time we changed that?"

"What are you suggesting?"

"Simple," said Kasri. "We bear letters for Lord Arandil. Let's see them delivered."

"Oh, yes. I'd forgotten. Let's summon the Forest Wardens, and we can hand them over."

A mischievous grin appeared on Kasri's face. "Or we could deliver them ourselves."

Herdwin paled. "I wouldn't advise that."

"Why? What's the worst that could happen?"

"They kill those who step off the trail, remember."

"Nonsense. I am successor to the Vard of Ironcliff, and you are a close advisor to the Queen of Merceria. Do you really believe they would risk a diplomatic incident?"

"Diplomatic incident? What do you think this is? A garden party? There are real consequences here."

Kasri moved to the middle of the trail and halted. "Come out," she shouted. "We know you're watching us. Show yourselves!"

Herdwin felt a fist clench his heart. He'd faced death in battle, taking wounds that would fell the toughest of Humans, but the thought of Kasri putting herself in danger was almost too much to bear. She was a brave warrior, even a dragon rider, yet her refusal to back down was the very thing that made her so. He feared this time it might be their undoing.

An Elf appeared, bow in hand. "Well?" he said, using the common tongue of the land. "I am here. What is it you wish to say?"

"We possess letters for Lord Arandil," said Kasri.

"Then give them to me, and I shall see them safely delivered."

"No. We are to deliver them in person. Take us to him."

"That is not our way."

"It is now."

"And who are you to make such demands? You are in our forest now, Dwarf, not the mountain home of your people."

"I am Kasri Ironheart, daughter of Thalgrun Stormhammer, Vard of Ironcliff, and successor to his Crown."

The Elf paused, appearing confused. Herdwin couldn't predict if the fellow would acquiesce or kill them, but his answer came soon enough.

"Very well, follow me." Without another word, the Forest Warden left the road, forcing the two Dwarves to hurry after him.

The thick underbrush in the woods didn't slow their guide. Several times the Dwarves halted, peering into the forest, trying to determine which way the Elf went. Eventually, they entered a clearing where their guide waited for them.

"Lord Arandil has agreed to meet you."

Herdwin looked around but saw no sign of any others. "And how do you know that?"

"I sent word ahead."

"With whom?"

The Elf laughed. "Have you not heard the calls of birds? We send messages over great distances by mimicking their cries."

"I don't mean to insult, but your people have the ears for it. We spend most of our time beneath rock and stone, hardly the place to develop such skills."

"Where are we to meet?" asked Kasri.

"I was instructed to take you to Thorolandrin, our home."

"Is that a city?"

"You would call it such."

"Then lead on, my friend. I'm eager to discover what an Elf city looks like."

The Elf ran off without a further word.

"Gundar's fist," said Herdwin. "Must they run everywhere?"

They raced after the fellow, soon finding themselves amongst the massive trunks again. The path, if one could call it that, took them on a meandering course defying all logic. As far as Herdwin could make out, they were moving in ever-decreasing circles. He couldn't help but wonder what lay at its centre.

The city took them both by surprise when it finally came into view. One moment dense underbrush surrounded them; the next, they walked along the leaf-strewn streets of Thorolandrin.

They both stared at the buildings in wonder, for they were made of shadowbark, a dark, thickly grained wood with the strength of steel. Many rested on pillars reaching high into the trees, while others blended seamlessly into the natural shape of the ground. Throughout it all, the sound of water in streams and fountains abounded.

"Look," said Kasri, pointing upward. "The roofs are all green. What are they made of?"

"Some kind of wood, I imagine. It seems to be all they build with around here. I wonder how these houses hold up in a storm?"

"Quite well, I should think. Shadowbark is sturdy."

"Yes," agreed Herdwin, "and expensive. Even the smallest of hovels appears to be built of the stuff. It would fetch a fortune in Wincaster."

"Do they export it, by chance?"

"No. From what I understand, the mages of Merceria possess a mirror made of shadowbark, but it's of ancient construction and likely dates back to the great migration."

"What migration was that?"

"The Mercerians' ancestors came to this land almost a thousand years ago as foreign mercenaries. That's how they got their name."

"Did they come from the east?"

"I believe they came by ship from the south."

"It must be strange to have a home that's barely a thousand years old."

"Indeed, but we can't all be Dwarves. Where would be the fun be in that?"

Their guide halted, then spread his arms wide to indicate the immediate area. "This is the gathering place. You must wait here, but do not wander far. The Lord of the Darkwood will soon bless you with his presence."

Herdwin looked at Kasri, who shrugged in response. The fellow had disappeared by the time he turned back. "Where did he go?"

They stood in a circular area, with a firepit in its centre, though not presently lit. Around the perimeter were what Herdwin first took to be stone steps, but upon closer examination, they led nowhere.

"What in the name of Gundar is this place?"

Kasri smiled. "Those are likely seats. I imagine people sit around the circle while others speak."

"If that's true, then this place would easily hold a hundred or more."

"And likely does. I know little of Elven customs, but I imagine all the important people gather here to make decisions."

"You mean nobles?"

"I don't know if they have such a thing. Perhaps they have guilds, like we do?"

"And the guild masters all come here?" said Herdwin. "It's an interesting concept. I wonder if they disagree as much as ours do?"

Kasri laughed. "Sometimes, I think arguing is all they know. I've seen them go at it for days on end over the smallest details. My father says it's the worst thing about being vard."

"What, arguing with the guild masters?"

"No, having to listen to them."

"Now, this looks interesting," said Herdwin as a trio of Elves entered the circle.

Two were guards, armed and armoured alike, while the third wore fine clothing and was the only one to speak. "Greetings. I am Shalariel, Mistress of Thorolandrin."

"Mistress?" said Kasri. "Does that mean you're in charge?"

"It does."

"Isn't Lord Arandil the ruler here?"

The Elf smiled. "I understand the confusion. Lord

Arandil rules the Kingdom of the Darkwood, while I look after this city."

"This city? You mean there are others?"

She chose not to answer. "Lord Arandil will be here momentarily. We thought it best I greet you first."

"I am Kasri Ironheart, daughter of—"

Shalariel raised her hand, cutting her off. "We know who you are." Her gaze turned to the smith. "And you, Herdwin Steelarm. We celebrate the accomplishments of both of you amongst our people. It is one of the reasons we decided to permit you entry to our city, but Lord Arandil will tell you more." She bowed, then moved aside as the Lord of the Darkwood approached.

"Greetings," he began. "It has been some time since we last met. I trust all is well?"

"More or less," said Herdwin. "We are travelling to Stonecastle on personal business, but there are some dispatches from Queen Anna to pass on to you."

"Yes," added Kasri, "but we never expected to be welcomed in an Elven city."

Lord Arandil smiled. "Yet that is precisely what you demanded." He waited for only a heartbeat before continuing. "It matters not. The times are changing, and we Elves must change with them. You are the first outsiders to gaze upon Thorolandrin. Tell me, what do you think?"

"It's beautiful," she replied. "What little we've seen of it."

"Then come. Let me show you the pride of the Darkwood."

"And the dispatches?"

"I will deal with them later; you and I both know there is nothing of consequence amongst them."

He led them out of the meeting place along a path paralleling a stream.

"So much water," said Herdwin. "It's strange to see it in the open like this."

"It is our very lifeblood. We designed the city from the beginning to worship nature, rather than reshape it."

"Would that we could do the same, but stone is unyielding and must be forced."

"Much like the temperament of your people," said the Elf Lord, though his smile revealed it a jest.

"Does that mean your people are more malleable?" asked Kasri.

"I see the Dwarves of Ironcliff are very astute. Come, I want to show you something." He led them up a flight of wooden stairs circling the trunk of a great tree. Soon, they were amongst the rooftops, gazing down at the city below.

"That stream runs through the centre of the city," explained Lord Greycloak, "but you can see where the tributaries meet it."

"And where does the water come from?" asked Herdwin.

"The mountains, for the most part, though there are lakes and ponds within the great forest that likewise feed it. This city has stood for over three thousand years, yet until now, only Elves have gazed upon it. We have always been an insular people, even more so since the rise of Kythelia, but with her defeat, it is time for us to take our place once more."

"As conquerors?"

"No, as friends to all who desire peace."

"That's mighty good to hear," said Kasri, "but I fear a little premature. Even as we speak, a great empire threatens the eastern border of Ironcliff. The Mercerians promised help, but where do you stand in that regard?"

"Our warriors will stand with our Mercerian allies. Where march their armies, so, too, march the Elves."

"That is most reassuring. I shall be sure to carry your words to my father."

"As you should." Lord Arandil stared off into the distance. "Your arrival here might prove beneficial to us both."

"In what way?"

"It just so happens one of our own is travelling to Stonecastle. I wonder if we might impose on you to permit him to accompany you?"

Kasri looked at Herdwin, who merely nodded. "Of course," she said. "Who is it?"

"Come. Let us break bread together first."

"I'm developing a taste for this wine," said Kasri. "Which is surprising, considering it's so mild."

"I shall arrange to send some to Wincaster," said Shalariel. "You can take it back to Ironcliff with you."

"Thank you. That would be most appreciated."

The Mistress of Thorolandrin turned her attention to Herdwin. "And you, Master Smith? What do you make of our fare?"

"Most delicious, although I do wonder why there is an empty seat at the table. Are we expecting someone?"

Shalariel cast her eyes down.

"That," explained Lord Arandil, "is in memory of our daughter, Telethial. She died at the hands of Norlanders."

"My apologies, Lord. I didn't mean to expose a vein."

"A vein?" said Shalariel. "What a curious expression."

"One our people often use," explained Kasri. "It refers to exposing a vein of ore unexpectedly."

"But surely that would be a good thing?"

"You would think so, wouldn't you, but our language sometimes has a strange way of twisting the meaning. I suppose you might use bringing up the past as an alternative?"

"It appears there is much for us to learn since we took refuge beneath the eaves of the Darkwood. Or maybe I should say relearn?"

"Our people have been on friendly terms for centuries," said Herdwin.

"Yet how much do we truly know of each other's ways? Take, for instance, this trip of yours to your ancestral home?"

"What of it?"

"You are in the company of a Dwarf of Ironcliff, are you not? That, alone, leads to idle speculation about the nature of your visit."

"We are going," said Kasri, "to try to settle a matter from the past. Herdwin's had some trouble with the smiths guild."

"Guild?" said Shalariel, turning to Lord Arandil.

"An organization of artisans or merchants united to

promote their services, oft times at the expense of outsiders."

"Aye," agreed Herdwin. "That about sums it up."

The Mistress of Thorolandrin was fascinated, even setting down her wine to concentrate on the conversation. "Does this mean you are not in good standing with the guild?"

"That's one way of putting it."

"Yet you are a master smith? How did that come about?"

"I mastered my trade years ago, but there were no openings. I decided to take my skills to Wincaster, where they'd be appreciated."

"He's smith to the Queen of Merceria," added Kasri.

"And a fine military commander, from what my husband tells me. Well done, Master Herdwin."

"Thank you, Mistress, or should I say, my lady?"

"Either will do."

Herdwin turned to Arandil. "My lord, you mentioned you had someone travelling to Stonecastle. Might I enquire as to who that would be?"

"That would be a relative of mine. A cousin, to use the terminology of your people."

"And his name?"

"Delsaran, a minstrel by trade, although I believe the term 'bard' is more appropriate in Merceria. He is going to Stonecastle to learn about your culture."

"And then?"

"Then he shall return and regale us with stories and songs."

"So, we are to be the subject of entertainment?"

"No, his role is to educate us. What better way than by words and music? Have you no similar role amongst your own people?"

"We have scholars," Herdwin replied, turning to Kasri. "What about Ironcliff?"

"We have musicians, but they play instruments, not sing, and definitely not for educational reasons. Singing for us is an expression of glee."

"Or sometimes sorrow," added Herdwin.

"Yes," said Shalariel. "Our people have their laments; it seems our cultures are not so different."

"When will we meet this Delsaran?"

"Not until you return to the road," said Lord Greycloak. "His presence can be a tad irritating at times."

"Irritating?"

"Pay no attention," said Shalariel. "My husband merely means he is apt to break into song at the drop of a hat."

"Lord Greycloak is?"

"No," said Kasri. "Delsaran. He's the bard, remember?"

Herdwin blushed. "Yes, of course. Pardon my confusion."

The Lord of the Darkwood laughed. "My irritation stems from my cousin's belief that our culture is not interesting enough. Thus, he feels the need to enrich it with his gifts."

"Is he good at it?"

"Admittedly, yes, but I shall deny it were he to ask. I believe praise should be used sparingly, else it spoils the effect."

"Have you enough food for the trip?" asked Shalariel. "I would not like to think we sent you on your way hungry."

"We're fine," said Kasri. "We stocked up on stonecakes before we left Wincaster but thank you for asking."

"When will you leave?"

"At first light—with your permission, of course."

"You are free to leave whenever you like," said Lord Arandil. "You do not need my permission. That said, we would be pleased to put you up for the night." He rose. "Now, if you will excuse me, I must retire. There are things I need to attend to."

Herdwin and Kasri both stood, bowing their heads respectfully.

"Thank you," said Kasri. "Both of you, for your hospitality. We shall forever be in your debt."

FIVE

On the Road

AUTUMN 966 MC

The mist did gather round about,
With dangers lurking near.
Yet ever onward, forth they went,
And overcame their fear.

Then distant peaks came into view,
The forest turned to hills.
And from on high came winter winds,
To give them both the chills.

T he mist clung to the ground like a warm winter blanket, while Herdwin paced back and forth on the trail, scanning the trees, or at least what he could see of them.

"This confounded fog is driving me to distraction. Where is this Delsaran fellow?"

"Take a breath," said Kasri. "He'll be along shortly. Maybe you should listen rather than watch?"

"Listen?"

"Yes. He is a bard after all. I'm sure we'll hear him singing as he approaches."

"You can't be serious?" He glanced at her only to witness a broad smile. "Very funny. Enjoying yourself?"

"I am and looking forward to heading into the mountains. You?"

"I have mixed emotions, if I'm being honest. It'll be nice to see my family, but then there's the guild to deal with, which is not the kind of thing I typically enjoy."

"How far is it to Stonecastle from here?"

"That's hard to say when I don't know where exactly 'here' is. Once we hit the foothills, it's only about thirty miles. Of course, that's as the raven flies. The path tends to wind about, primarily because of the rough terrain. Is that anything like Ironcliff?"

"No. Ironcliff opens directly onto a plain, although you have to go up a long set of stairs to get to the entrance."

"Not defensive terrain, then."

"No, but it has the advantage of growing an abundance of crops. Just out of curiosity, once we do arrive, who do we visit first?"

"My cousin Gelion," replied Herdwin. "And then the vard. I can't very well visit without involving him."

"And what is your vard like?"

Herdwin chuckled. "He's not 'my vard' anymore, not since I moved to Wincaster."

"Still, do you get along? He must trust you, or he wouldn't have put you in charge of his warriors?"

"Aye, he trusts me. Vard Khazad and I go way back."

"Is he a cousin?"

"No, but I spent several months under his supervision during my apprentice phase."

"You mentioned trying the carpenters guild; are there any others you spent time with?"

"Yes, the miners and the engineers. The guild of engineers recommended me to the smiths guild, said I possessed a gift for working with my hands."

"And which one did Vard Khazad supervise?"

"The miners," replied Herdwin, "but he wasn't the vard back then, merely a senior guild member."

"You must've made quite an impression."

"He and I got along famously, but we both realized I wasn't suited to the work. We've kept in touch ever since, though."

"Was he vard when you left the guild?"

"He was, but he hadn't held the Throne for long. He tried to intervene on my behalf, but you know how stubborn guild masters can be."

"Do you think he'll help you now?"

"Perhaps," said Herdwin. "He's sat on the Throne for over half a century and learned a few things, I'll warrant. The question is, can he actually do anything? The vards of Stonecastle possess limited power regarding the guilds."

"Yet unlimited power in other things," mused Kasri. "It's the same back in Ironcliff."

A voice called out from the mist, "Am I interrupting?"

They both turned to see a slender Elf emerging from the trees, dressed in green and yellow, with a dark, hooded cloak resting on his shoulders.

"Allow me to introduce myself. I am Delsaran." He bowed, an action that would've looked more at home in the court of kings.

"I'm Herdwin, and this is Kasri. You're coming to Stonecastle with us, I believe?"

"I am, to see old 'One-Eye' himself."

"You'd do better to refer to him as Vard Khazad. He doesn't much like being reminded of his loss."

"My mistake. I shall remember that in future. Are we ready to get underway?"

"By all means," said Herdwin.

Dwarves, being a short-statured race, typically walked at a slower speed than Elves or Humans, which soon became apparent to their travelling companion as they made their way eastward.

"So," began the Elf, "tell me about yourselves."

Herdwin grumbled something unintelligible, causing Kasri to chuckle. "What would you like to know?" she asked.

"Well, you could start by telling me why you two are travelling together. Are you bonded?"

"Bonded is an Orc term, not Dwarven."

"I stand corrected. Still, the question remains unanswered."

"We are not forged, if that's what you're asking. We are,

at the moment, merely friends travelling in each other's company. Surely you've seen Dwarves before?"

"I have, though not one of the female persuasion."

Kasri laughed.

"You find something amusing?" he said.

"My pardon," said Kasri, "but you know little of the mountain folk."

"Meaning?"

"You've probably seen many female Dwarves; you just didn't realize it."

"How could that possibly be?"

"I assume, from your manner, you've witnessed Dwarven warriors marching through the Darkwood?"

"I have. What of it?"

"Would it surprise you to know female Dwarves were amongst them?"

"Impossible!"

"Why would you say that?"

"They all had beards."

"That's what they want you to believe."

"Now I am confused," said Delsaran. "Are you saying the females of your race all have beards?"

"No, but they wear one when marching to war. The better to confuse our enemies. They're usually attached to the helmet."

"Astounding. I would never have believed it."

"Your own race sends women to fight. I saw them in battle."

"Yes, but I had no idea the mountain folk were so enlightened."

"He thinks we're barbarians," grumbled Herdwin.

"Not barbarians," defended the Elf. "Merely different in your own unique way."

"Is that supposed to sound less like an insult? Because if it is, it failed miserably."

"My pardon. Perhaps I ought to take the lead? I know this part of the Darkwood well."

"That would be much appreciated."

After another day, they emerged from the Darkwood to massive mountain peaks in the distance. To the Dwarves, it was nothing unusual, but their companion had other thoughts.

"By the Goddess, I have never seen anything like that before."

"Have you never wandered to the forest's edge?" asked Kasri.

"Why would I? I am a troubadour, a singer of songs, not some adventurous soul. My place is amongst civilized people."

"Are you suggesting Herdwin and I aren't civilized?"

The Elf blushed. "No. At least, that is not what I intended. I merely meant to suggest there are none as cultured as the Elves, for we have had thousands of years to perfect life."

"Careful now," warned Herdwin. "Us mountain folk have been around just as long as your lot."

A twig snapped, then a branch moved off to their right,

and when they turned to look, they saw a great boar emerge from the underbrush, charging straight for them.

Herdwin had his axe out in no time, while Kasri pulled forth Stormhammer. Despite possessing a sword, Delsaran backed up, his face paling as he caught sight of the beast. It headed straight for Herdwin, but the smith stood his ground, axe at the ready. Kasri pointed the hammer at the creature, letting loose with a bolt of lightning that arced out but hit the ground, narrowly missing the target.

Delsaran shrieked as Herdwin swung a low blow aimed at the creature's head, but the thick skull proved impervious to his weapon. A tusk smashed into the Dwarf's side, knocking him to the ground while the boar continued past him.

Kasri ran towards him but kept her eyes on the vicious beast as it turned around for another charge. She lowered the hammer again, the lightning striking true this time, felling the boar in its tracks.

"I'm all right," called out Herdwin. "It only hit my mail." He rose, feeling his side with one hand. "That's going to leave a nasty bruise."

"That was incredible!" shouted Delsaran.

Both Dwarves looked around but saw no signs of the Elf.

"Where are you?" called out Kasri.

"Up here, in the trees." The bard dropped to the ground. "It is always best to put some height between oneself and the enemy, do you not think?"

"A little hard to strike back, isn't it? Especially considering you don't have a bow."

Delsaran straightened his tunic. "I am an entertainer, not

a warrior. Still, that hammer of yours is an impressive weapon. Might I ask where it came from?"

"A smith," said Kasri. "Where else?"

"Come now. Even I know hammers do not usually throw lightning. You need magic for that."

"It's an heirloom, passed down through generations."

"Impressive. You must be a Dwarf of some renown to possess such a weapon."

"Did Lord Arandil not tell you who we are?"

"No, I cannot say he did. Why? Are you someone important?"

"No," interrupted Herdwin. "That is to say, we're no more important than any other individual."

"But she has a magic weapon?"

"Yes, she does, but such things are common amongst our people."

"They are?" whispered Kasri.

Herdwin lowered his voice. "It is, as far as he's concerned."

"But why don't we tell him who we are?"

"And have him singing it all over the place? That's hardly going to help me with the guild."

"You make a good point."

"What are you two whispering about?" called out Delsaran.

"Nothing," replied Herdwin. "Just speculating on where the boar came from."

The Elf approached cautiously, his gaze locked on the body of the creature. "Are you sure it is dead?"

"If it's not, it's doing a fine job of pretending."

Delsaran jumped back, his hand going to the hilt of his sword. "They can do that?"

"No," said Kasri. "Now, let's leave this place before we lose the sun."

"A pity," said Herdwin. "A nice piece of roast boar would've gone down well."

"True, but we haven't the time for it. And the last thing we want is to carry a carcass through the mountain passes."

"Yes, I suppose you're right. Very well, let's continue, shall we?"

"Wait," said the Elf. "You kill that thing and just continue on the way as if nothing happened?"

"What else would you have us do?" asked Kasri.

"Let me think… offer a prayer to Tauril?"

"And why would we do that?"

"She is the goddess of the woods. Surely, of all the Gods, she is the one we must appease?"

"Appease? Do you suppose the Gods stand around all day watching us mere mortals?"

"Yes, of course. Are you saying they do not?"

"Not in the least. You must think yourself important if you believe that."

"I like to think of myself as devout, if I understand you correctly."

"Well, devout or not, we still need to be on our way. There's miles to go before we reach the first tower."

"Tower?" said Delsaran. "No one ever said anything about towers."

"Actually," said Kasri, "Herdwin mentioned it previously, but you weren't here to hear it."

"It hardly counts if I was not present!"

She turned to her fellow Dwarf. "He seems to believe we have a duty to explain everything to him."

Herdwin scowled. "He better get used to it, or it's going to be a long trip." They both turned to continue eastward.

Delsaran hurried to catch up. "Are there likely to be more creatures like that up in the mountains?"

"No," replied Herdwin. "Boars don't live there. Now, bears, on the other hand…"

The terrain grew rougher, the trees falling away to either side and then, before long, they were making their way up an incline. Kasri and Herdwin kept their pace, but the Elf soon struggled.

"How in the name of the Gods can you move so fast? This is killing me."

Herdwin allowed himself a quick glance at the Elf. "Have you never climbed a hill before?"

"Naturally, but this is far more than just a hill."

"Well, it continues like this for quite some time. Do you need a rest?"

"Yes," said Delsaran, relief in his voice.

"Good. Then we'll stop when we reach that rock up ahead."

The Elf peered upward. "I see no rock."

Herdwin pointed. "It's right there, beneath that cliff face, where the path runs along the base."

"But that is miles away!"

"Not to a Dwarf."

"Actually," said Kasri, ignoring the Elf, "the distance doesn't change because we're Dwarves."

"True, but such a distance is of little consequence to us."

"Oh," said the Elf. "Are you just going to ignore me now?"

"Did you hear something?" asked Kasri.

"Probably the wind," replied Herdwin. "Pay it no mind."

"We should let the poor fellow rest. It wouldn't do to arrive with him in a state of exhaustion."

"Very well, but at this rate, it's going to take us forever to get there."

They found some level ground and sat.

"Shall we build a fire?" asked Delsaran.

"For what?" said Herdwin. "We're only resting."

"Why, to cook food, of course."

"And what food would that be?"

"I… I just assumed you travelled with rations."

"And so, we do. Don't you?"

The Elf's face fell. "This is all so new to me."

Herdwin stared at him before finally pulling his pack closer and rummaging through it. Moments later, he produced what looked like a lump of charcoal. "Here. Try this."

Delsaran took it, giving it a sniff. "What is it?"

"A stonecake."

The bard tried to bite off a piece. "And well named it is. How am I supposed to eat it?"

"You let it sit in your mouth a bit. Your spit will soften it."

"And then?"

"Then you chew it and swallow. What else?"

Delsaran placed the morsel into his mouth, then waited. He smiled as the flavour took hold.

"He's got it," said Kasri.

The Elf chewed away, then asked, "Could I have another?"

"Another?" said Herdwin. "That's a meal's worth."

"Really? But hunger still gnaws at me."

"Give it time to reach your stomach."

They sat there for a bit, and then Delsaran rubbed his belly. "Oh my, I see what you mean. Perhaps I should have chewed it some more. You say that lasts a day?"

"No, one meal. You'll need another tonight."

"And you can live on these?"

"Dwarves can," said Herdwin. "I don't know about Elves, but Humans can only eat them for so long before they get ill."

"Ill? Are you suggesting these stonecakes will kill me?"

"No, but Humans require things they can't provide."

"Like what?"

Herdwin shrugged. "How would I know? I'm not a healer."

"As long as we're resting," said Kasri, "how about a song? You are a bard, are you not?"

"I am," said Delsaran, "but this is hardly the place for such frivolity."

"Nonsense. A song would go a long way to giving us strength to continue, don't you think?"

"I cannot argue with your logic. Very well, I shall repay your gift of food with a song. Have you any song, in particular, you would care to hear?"

"I doubt you know any Dwarven ones."

"Good point," said the Elf. "How about I pick one of my own people's songs?"

"Sounds like a good idea."

Delsaran cleared his throat before humming a bit to figure out the tune. "This is the story of Telethial," he announced. "It is a lament." When he finally began, his dulcet tones drifted across to them like a gentle summer breeze.

"Telethial, they called her, morning star to one and all
And never was a heart so pure until her fateful fall.

Upon the lands of men she trod, her sword hand held up high,
Until that fateful strike rang true and sent her to the sky.

Yet still her spirit wanders here, amongst the boughs so dark,
Her voice to speak no more of home, no more to leave her mark.

Her golden smile, her laughter clear, her azure eyes so blue,
Enchanted all who came within her many-layered view.

So sing with me in praise to her who walks the land no more,
And think of her, Telethial, who walked in days of yore."

. . .

"Very nice," said Kasri.

"Yes," agreed Herdwin. "It's clear you loved her a lot."

The Elf blushed. "She was loved by all, for she was the fairest of Elves."

"Yet your voice would indicate more. Tell me, was she aware of your love for her?"

"She was," said Delsaran, "though she did not reciprocate. She was marvellous, gracious to all, regardless of background."

"That must've been difficult for you," said Kasri. "How long did you know her?"

"Only a few centuries, yet it feels like my entire life."

"Sorry. Did you say a few centuries?"

"I did."

"How old are you?"

"Just over twelve hundred years. Why?"

"How is it you only knew her for a few centuries? Didn't you both grow up in Thorolandrin?"

"No. I only came to that city in my later years. Before that, I lived in..." His voice trailed off. "Sorry. We are forbidden to speak of such things."

"I'm guessing you were about to name another Elf city," said Herdwin. "Just how many are there in the Darkwood?"

"I am not at liberty to say."

"Very well, I'll not press you for further details right now."

SIX

Into the Mountains

Up the forlorn tower,
With its Dwarven, strong-built stone.
And then, along the crooked path,
They walked, but not alone.

For with them went the hope of all,
Who fear to tread unknown.
And at the end, there waited king,
Upon his Dwarven Throne.

T wo days later, Kasri spotted a tall, grey structure up against the side of an immense cliff.

"What's that?" she asked.

"That," replied Herdwin, "is the forlorn tower."

"It's a strange design for a defensive structure."

"Ah, but it's so much more than that."

"Meaning?"

"It has two exits, one near the ground and the other atop that cliff."

"Are there stairs inside?"

"No, although there is a ladder in case the mechanism fails."

"Mechanism?" said Delsaran. "What in the Gods name is that?"

"A lift," said Herdwin. "The miracle that is Dwarven engineering. The tower's base is wide enough to admit a large wagon, minus the horses, of course."

"To what end?"

"That's where the engineering comes in. Using a system of counterweights and gears, it lifts the entire floor to the top of the cliff. Then they just pull the wagon out."

"And the horses?"

"They go up on a separate trip. It's quite remarkable."

"Is the tower manned?" asked Delsaran.

"Aye, there's a garrison who can easily disable the lift, thus preventing it from being used to attack. Look closely at the top; you'll see where the battlements overhang the entire structure."

"And how would they use their arbalests at such a steep angle?"

"That's the beauty of it—they don't need to. Even a small rock would be lethal from such a height."

"Fascinating," said the Elf. "But how do we inform them we want to go up?"

"In times of peace, warriors are stationed at the bottom. I'll introduce you once we're closer."

Kasri kept staring at the tower. "An impressive fortification, even without the lift. How did they build it so high without its foundation crumbling under the weight?"

Herdwin smiled. "I see you know something about engineering. The fact is, they used magic to fuse the stones."

"They did? It doesn't look like it."

"That's just for show. After all, a Dwarf can't have their work looking ugly now, can they?"

They spotted a trio of Dwarves at the tower's base. One dozed in a chair by the door while the other two tended a pot steaming away over a fire.

"Greetings," called out Herdwin.

A grin broke out on one of the guardian's faces. "Ah, Master Herdwin. It's been some time since we saw your smiling face around here." He advanced to greet them but stopped cold, his hand going to the hilt of his sword. "Who's this?"

"Friends," replied Herdwin. "This is Kasri of Ironcliff and Delsaran, an Elven bard."

The guard relaxed. "I'm Taldur, and this is Grolik."

Kasri bowed. "Pleased to meet you." She nodded at the door. "Who is the slumbering fellow?"

"Rotmir, but all he ever does is sleep." He let his gaze linger on Kasri momentarily before bowing deeply. "It is rare to see a female Dwarf on the road, especially one unbearded. To what do we owe the pleasure?"

"I am travelling to Stonecastle with Herdwin. Why else

would I be on this road? Unless there's more to the east than a Dwarven stronghold?"

Grolik barked out a laugh. "Hah. She has you there, Taldur!"

Kasri ignored the outburst. "I understand this is the famous forlorn tower. Might I ask how it got its name?"

"Aye. Well," mumbled Taldur, "that has more to do with its location than anything else. Let's just say that, as a warrior, it's a miserable place to spend your time."

"We didn't always call it that," said Grolik. "It used to be the Tower of Might."

"No, it didn't," replied Taldur. He turned his attention back to Kasri. "Ignore him. He doesn't know what he's talking about." He looked over at Herdwin. "I heard you did rather well for yourself in the recent war. Have you returned to share your knowledge?"

"No. I'm going to see the vard."

"He won't help you. The guilds have been giving him a hard time."

"Over what?"

"His plans to build a stronger army. Of course, the warriors guild agrees with him, but they don't control the purse strings."

"It's an old argument," said Herdwin. "Every time we finish a war, there's talk of reducing our fighting complement. You'd think they'd learn something from centuries of history."

"You and I both know that," said Taldur, "but the common folk forget. In their eyes, the war in Merceria was distant and of little interest. Many questioned why we sent any warriors in the first place."

"We had to, if only to have a seat at the table."

"Table?" said Grolik.

"He's talking about the Mercerians," replied his companion. "If I recall, we got trade concessions from them."

"Yes," said Herdwin, "and that, I'm sure, has made the guilds more profitable."

"It has, but not so much that they're content to let some of those coins spill over to the vard."

"So Khazad is besieged?"

"You might say that."

Herdwin turned to Kasri. "Is there this problem back in Ironcliff?"

"No, but we face a more immediate threat to the east. There's nothing like a nearby enemy to unite the mountain folk."

"If only we had such a threat," said Taldur, "but Herdwin here had to go and make friends with the Mercerians. Who's left to threaten us now?"

The smith laughed. "You could always go to war with the Elves of the Darkwood?"

"What?" cried out Delsaran. "You cannot be serious? Even to suggest such a thing is ludicrous."

"Calm yourself. I speak only in jest."

Once more, Kasri stared up at the tower. "This is an impressive structure. How long did it take to construct?"

"Years," replied Taldur. "It replaced an old rope-and-sling contraption. Mind you, back in those days, the warriors guarding it had no shelter."

"Were you alive then?"

"No, of course not. That was centuries ago. "He looked up in wonderment. "We no longer have masters of stone to make things like this anymore; our days of glory are gone."

"I never knew you to be so gloomy," said Herdwin.

"It's this place; it wears on a fellow." Taldur stared at the group before suddenly shifting his feet. "My pardon. Here we are chatting away, and I forget my duty. Would you like to ascend?"

"Yes, thank you."

"Then come this way, and we'll send you up." He led them to the waiting double doors, then pulled one open, revealing a large chamber. "You'll want to hold on to a handrail," he said, nodding at a side. "The ride can get a little bumpy at times."

Kasri grasped one firmly with both hands. "How do they know when it's time to raise the lift?"

Taldur closed the door, sealing the four of them inside. "I'll notify them." He moved to one side where a horn sat and lifted it to his lips, blowing out three clear notes. After a brief delay, the floor vibrated momentarily before the entire room shook as it began its climb.

"How long does this take?" asked Kasri.

"With only the four of us? Not long. Wagons, however, require us to engage additional gears, which slows it down quite a bit."

"This is frightening," said Delsaran. "A room should not move about like this. It is unnatural."

"You're welcome to take the ladder," offered Taldur.

The Elf paled. "On second thought, this is not as bad as I expected."

"This is remarkable," said Kasri. "Are there some to the east of Stonecastle as well?"

"There are towers, but nothing like this. The terrain there isn't suited to it."

"Are you saying there are no cliffs?"

"Oh, there are cliffs all right," said Taldur, "but none that need traversing. The path eastward winds through the mountains. The only real obstacle is the bridge."

"What bridge is that?"

"They call it Kharzun's Folly because of the tremendous expense."

"Was Kharzun the Dwarf who designed it?"

"No," replied Taldur. "He's the vard who insisted on building it in the first place. Of course, it wasn't called Kharzun's Folly till years later."

"I'm afraid I'm not following?"

"The trade to the east never materialized. They wasted all those coins building it, and the guilds weren't happy. It's what led them to take over the realm's finances."

"And how long ago was this?" asked Kasri.

"Five centuries," replied Taldur, "give or take a decade. Do the guilds control the treasury in Ironcliff?"

"No, though they've suggested it. They seem to believe they're the only ones capable of overseeing such things."

"The guilds were good in their day," said Herdwin, "but now they stifle us instead of allowing us to grow."

"Careful," warned Taldur. "Such talk would not be popular in Stonecastle, particularly if any guilds hear of it."

"I'll bear that in mind."

The room shook one final time, then went still.

"We're here," announced their host.

The door swung outward, revealing the top of the cliff, along with a road running eastward.

"There you go," said Taldur. "What did you think?"

Kasri smiled. "The ride was most illuminating. Thank you."

They stepped outside, to dark clouds hanging over the mountains and a wind that had picked up considerably.

"Perhaps we should seek shelter for the night," suggested Herdwin.

"No. Let us continue. I'm eager to see Stonecastle."

"We won't reach it tonight."

"I know, but at least we'll be closer."

"And if it rains?"

"Then we get wet. I can handle a little discomfort if it speeds our progress."

"A Dwarf after my own heart," replied Herdwin, then blushed as his words sank in. He stumbled to apologize. "What I meant was..."

"I understand what you meant, and I take no offence." She smiled. "Then again, you're not entirely wrong to think otherwise." She took his hand in hers. "Come. Let's walk hand in hand as the Humans do."

They proceeded thus for a dozen steps, then released their hold. "Never mind. It's an awkward custom."

"Agreed," said Herdwin. "I'm not sure how they manage it, for it interferes with my gait."

"As it does mine. Still, I suppose it would be pleasant if we were strolling down the streets of Wincaster."

"Agreed, yet not so for a trip such as this."

"Did I miss something?" asked Delsaran, running to catch up.

Both Dwarves blushed.

"Ah," said the Elf. "Now I understand."

"Then I would ask you to remain silent on the matter," said Herdwin. "There are those in Stonecastle who might use our relationship against me."

"You have my word. I shall remain mute on the subject once we reach our destination. Might I enquire as to how you two met? I only ask out of professional curiosity."

"We both led warriors during the war. The Mercerians created one brigade of Dwarves."

"Brigade? That must be a Human term."

"Unique to the Mercerians, as far as I'm aware. They considered it best to put all us Dwarves together to take advantage of our strengths."

"And so you fought side by side, truly the making of an epic love song. I shall add it to the ballad of the mountain folk."

"You will not!" said Herdwin. "You promised to remain silent on the matter."

"I would obviously change the names, but I cannot hide away such a tale from the good people of Eiddenwerthe. Such stories deserve to be told in all their glory."

"Not in Stonecastle, they don't. You put me in a difficult position here, Master Elf."

"That being?"

"I've never had cause to threaten the life of an Elf, yet you try my patience."

"What he means," said Kasri, "is you can speak of this no more, and that includes in song."

"But just think of it; your names immortalized for all the ages."

"You just said you'd change our names. Come now, which is it?"

The Elf's face fell. "Very well, but I do so only under protest."

"Noted," said Herdwin.

As they camped on a ledge that night, Herdwin fell asleep quickly, but Delsaran kept fidgeting, keenly aware should he roll over in his sleep, he might plummet to his death.

With the coming of morning, the two Dwarves, and the slightly dishevelled Elf, got on their way once more. The road slowly curved around the side of a mountain, but by noon, they could finally make out the distant walls of Stonecastle.

"There it is," said Herdwin. "The jewel of the Dwarves. We founded the city after the discovery of a great silver deposit over three thousand years ago. Naturally, we mined out that particular vein centuries ago, but they still work the deep mines."

"For gold?" asked Kasri.

"No, mostly silver these days, though some iron deposits are at the deeper levels."

"Just how deep do the mines go?" asked the Elf.

"They make the forlorn tower look small in comparison. In fact, they pump air down there to stop the miners from passing out."

"How does one pump air?"

"Through a series of large bellows," said Herdwin, "much like a smith uses."

"Do they work the bellows all day long?"

"No, the entire thing is made up of gears and... never mind. It's clearly beyond your understanding."

"All fascinating stuff," said Delsaran, "but of little consequence in the grand scheme of things."

"Not to those who work the mines."

"You make an excellent point."

"Does Stonecastle have a single entrance?" asked Kasri.

"There's the main one we'll go through and then a few escape tunnels to flee should that become necessary. They're sealed off from the outside but would be opened in an emergency."

"I find it hard to imagine what kind of trouble would require abandoning the city."

"You'd be surprised. They almost activated them some sixty years ago."

"You were attacked?"

"No, the miners unearthed an elemental. The thing panicked and went on a rampage until they finally coaxed it back into the deep."

"What is 'the deep'?" asked Delsaran.

"I know that," said Kasri. "Deep below the ground or mountains, in this case, are tunnels that go on for hundreds of miles. No one knows where they go or what created them, or maybe I should say who?"

"Have they ever been explored?"

"Not to my knowledge, but perhaps Herdwin can tell us more?"

"I wish I could, but information is sparse. The air down there is foul, and even with ventilation, it oft times requires magic to breathe. It's also stiflingly hot. We learned all about the dangers of the deep when I apprenticed to the miners."

"Are you not a smith?" asked Delsaran.

"I was, or rather I am, but when we Dwarves come of age, we try several trades before deciding on our life's work. We refer to each as an apprenticeship."

"And how many does a typical Dwarf try?"

"That depends," said Herdwin. "Some are lucky and pick the correct career right off the mark. Others, like me, spend years trying different guilds before settling on one. What's the Elven custom?"

"We tend not to specialize. I suppose it is only natural, considering how long we live. I mean, who wants to do the same thing for a thousand years?"

"But you must have trades, surely? Who produces your armour and weapons?"

"You seem to be under the mistaken idea those are things constantly in demand. There have been no new births in the Darkwood for centuries. Who would require weapons that do not already possess them?"

"Weapons still break or get damaged."

"Yes, and there are always a few individuals who dedicate a century or so to such pursuits. I am afraid your concept of guilds would not work amongst my people."

"Fascinating," said Herdwin, "yet it explains so much."

"Are you speaking of generalities?" asked Kasri. "Or thinking of something specific?"

"I remember talking to Gerald about Kythelia's army—the living ones, not the spirits. He said they'd learned nothing about fighting in more than a thousand years. Now I see why; they're a stagnant race. Sorry, Delsaran. I don't mean that in a negative way, but your people adapt slowly to change."

"I cannot deny it," said the Elf, "but there appears to be a change of heart of late brought about by the loss of Telethial. Lord Arandil is determined to see our people prosper."

"As should all rulers."

"And Vard Khazad? What is he like?"

"He wants what is best for his people, but he's surrounded by those who only have their own self-interest at heart."

"It is a common problem. Even amongst the Elves, some serve only themselves. It is, I think, the nature of all living beings, or at least the civilized ones."

"Well," said Herdwin, "you'll see plenty of selfish folk in Stonecastle."

"And have you any advice on that matter?"

"Yes. Guard your words carefully. Others can often twist them to cause problems for you."

"Is it that bad?" asked Kasri.

"At court, definitely. Of course, outside of that, feel free to speak your mind. Dwarves have a tradition of offering their opinions freely, whether or not they are wanted. They say the biggest arguments are the most productive, and the guild masters have perfected that to a fine art. Khazad himself once told me it took three days for the guild masters to agree on an agenda. Three days! Can you imagine?"

"Surely he was exaggerating?"

"No. I don't believe so, but I tell you what, let's ask when we meet him."

SEVEN

Stonecastle

AUTUMN 966 MC

The mighty fortress at the mount,
Stonecastle was its name.
And there, within those hallowed halls,
Awaited Herdwin's fame.

But all is not forgiven,
In the land of mountain folk.
And our poor hero, master smith,
Must throw off Dwarf guild's yoke.

T wo immense towers flanked the gates of Stonecastle, each bristling with giant bolt throwers, larger versions of their famed arbalests. The city's massive shadowbark doors, reinforced by steel bands, were covered with a substance that warded off the effects of weather and time.

The process gave them a glistening effect as if they were freshly painted.

Within these doors was a smaller one, more suited for individuals than wagons. Herdwin had passed by city guards many times, but while those of Human towns tended to be bored and uninterested in visitors, these of Stonecastle were far different.

As the travellers approached, the door opened, disgorging half a dozen warriors, two carrying arbalests loaded and aimed at the new arrivals, causing Delsaran to pause.

"Is this how your people welcome visitors?"

"This is not their normal behaviour," replied Herdwin. "Something has them on edge."

"Halt where you are," came the command.

They did as they were bid. The Dwarven guard approached, and their leader, a dour-looking individual with a red beard, rested his gaze on Herdwin. "I recognize you, Master Herdwin, but your companions are strangers here."

"Then allow me to introduce them. This is Kasri Iron-heart, a Dwarf of Ironcliff, and this is Delsaran of the Darkwood."

The guard turned his attention to the Elf. "What is your purpose here?"

"I come at the behest of Lord Greycloak to learn more about your people."

"And you?" said the guard, his gaze on Kasri.

"I am here as a friend of Herdwin Steelarm."

"So, you came to meet his family?"

"I have," she replied. "Why? Is that strange?"

"Not at all, Mistress Kasri, though admittedly, it is rare. I can't recall the last time a Dwarven outsider travelled here."

"Are you satisfied our presence here represents no threat to your kingdom?"

"I am." The guard waved his warriors to lay down their weapons. "Let me be the first to welcome you to Stonecastle." He held out his hand, and Herdwin took it in a firm grip. "I trust I've not offended you?"

"You were only doing your job," replied the smith. "One can never be faulted for that, but tell me, why all the fuss? This is not the usual welcome I've come to expect."

"There's been trouble in the east."

"Is it serious?"

"Serious enough to put the guard on alert. Other than that, I know nothing." The leader of the guards ushered them inside before following them.

"Thank you," said Herdwin. "I shall be sure to mention your attention to duty."

"You are most kind."

Herdwin led them into the streets of the outer city.

"All this stone," mused the Elf. "Have you no wood in Stonecastle?"

"What kind of question is that? Do you see trees growing anywhere?"

"None whatsoever, but the stone gives the whole place such a gloomy atmosphere."

"Gloomy?" said Kasri. "I would've said quite the opposite. Stone has such a warm feel to it, wouldn't you say?"

"Indeed," replied Herdwin. "Now, shall I show you the

outer city first, or do we go directly to the home of my cousin Gelion?"

"I believe the city would be most appropriate. I'd be interested to see how it differs from Ironcliff. What of you, Master Elf? What will you do now that we've arrived?"

"I must say my goodbyes," said Delsaran. "Though I would be much obliged if you could point me in the direction of the Royal Court?"

"Head towards the mountain," replied Herdwin. "You'll find what you're looking for in what we call 'the mount', which rests beneath the stone itself."

"Thank you. I hope we meet again. The journey was pleasant, not to mention an eye-opening experience. I do, however, feel there is much more to learn."

"And you will be well-placed to do so at the court of Vard Khazad. Fear not. We shall meet again, though it may not be for several days."

Delsaran headed north towards the mountainside that stood watch over the outer city.

"What do you think?" asked Kasri. "Will the vard welcome him?"

"Had you asked me that ten years ago, I would've said no, but recent events have taught the Dwarves of Stonecastle to be more accepting of others."

"The Dwarves of Stonecastle? Do you not count yourself amongst them?"

"Part of me will always miss this place, but my home is in Wincaster now, has been for over fifty years. If I'm being honest, I don't think I could ever return here to live. It appears I've become accustomed to the presence of Humans."

"But this was your home."

"You know, a good friend of mine once told me home isn't a place; it's a feeling you get when surrounded by loved ones."

"Did Gelion tell you that?"

"No, Gerald Matheson."

"The Marshal of Merceria?"

"Yes. Does that surprise you?"

"It most certainly does," said Kasri. "I'll admit he's a brilliant strategist, but I never took him for a philosopher."

"I'm sure he'd be the first to deny it, but I know him, and I stand by my claim."

"As you should. Now, tell me about the outer city. Do they grow crops here?"

"They do," replied Herdwin. "Though they're not much to look at. The road we're on leads straight to the mount, while the side streets form a grid pattern. Each group of buildings surrounds a central courtyard where they grow various crops. If you look carefully, you can see them through the space between buildings."

"What do they grow?"

"Primarily carrots, peas, turnips, and of course, potatoes. They brought the soil up from the various valleys and streams around the area."

"That must have taken forever."

"It did. Centuries, in fact. Of course, these are only supplemental. The primary food sources in Stonecastle are all grown underground."

"Let me guess, fungus?"

"Yes, quite a variety, but we also raise goats, and many of the underground pools are teeming with fish."

"Would that be clearfish?"

"Mainly, but some other varieties as well. Do you have them in Ironcliff?"

"We do," she replied. "Clearfish is known as a delicacy back home. Here?"

"It's as common as rainwater. The guilds perfected the art of farming fish so well it's now one of our staples."

Kasri halted, looking inside a carpenter shop as they passed by. "So, you do have some trees?"

"Naturally, we could hardly make everything out of stone, but I wasn't going to tell the Elf that. Having said that, wooden items fetch a steep price here."

"You could probably make a fortune by shipping in logs."

"Likely, but who would want all that work to get them here?"

"We made it easy enough."

"Yes," said Herdwin, "but it won't be long until winter settles in, and then any thoughts of travel come to a halt."

"Why? Are the winters here severe?"

"That's putting it mildly. I remember once when I was a child, it got so cold they abandoned the outer city for a few days."

"That must've been awful."

Herdwin shrugged. "I thought of it as a big adventure, but I was too young to know better."

"Perhaps we should visit your cousin now?"

"Very well. It's down this way."

. . .

As was the Dwarven custom, Gelion Brightaxe's house consisted of two storeys—the main living area and the lower floor sleeping quarters, dug beneath the rock. It was a fairly typical design from the outside, with irregular-shaped stones held in place by a mixture of mortar and a roof covered by overlapping slate tiles.

They didn't even make it as far as the door before a voice called out, "Herdwin, is that you?"

"It is," he replied. "And I've brought company."

A female Dwarf appeared at the door, her leather apron covered in fine stone dust. "Who's this, now?"

"Kasri Ironheart. She hails from Ironcliff. I hope we're not interrupting."

"Not at all. I was cutting some stone, but it can wait."

"And Gelion?"

"On duty, of course. His company is on the wall today, but you'll see him later. Come in, and we'll break out the ale. You must be dying of thirst."

She led them inside, beckoning them to sit beside the hearth as she retrieved some tankards.

"You have a nice home," said Kasri.

"Thank you."

"They're both well-placed in their respective guilds," said Herdwin. "Margel here is a senior master of the stone guild, while Gelion holds a captaincy."

"That means you outrank him," said Kasri. "After all, you commanded several companies during the war."

"Yes, but it was Mercerian rank and only temporary at that."

"Still, it accounts for something, surely?"

"Here's your ale," said Margel, handing out the tankards. She took off her apron and sat, placing her feet on a small footstool. "So, what brings you to Stonecastle? Not that we're not pleased to see you, of course, but it's not every day you choose to make the trip."

"We're here on business," said Herdwin. "Or at least, I am. Kasri agreed to come with me to keep me company."

"Oh yes? And how did you two meet?"

"During the war."

"War?"

"Yes, the war between the Human realms?"

"Oh, that. Yes. The vard sent warriors, but other than that, we've heard little."

Kasri smiled. "There were dragons."

"Now you're pulling my leg," said Margel. "There haven't been dragons in these parts for thousands of years."

"The Kurathians brought them."

"Kurathians?"

"Yes," said Herdwin. "Human mercenaries from across the sea. And as for the dragons, Kasri is being humble. She rode one of them."

"Along with others," added his companion. "I couldn't have done it all by myself."

"I'm impressed," said their host. "I never met a dragon rider before. Where is this beast now?"

"Far to the north, in the Thunder Mountains near my home. Have you ever heard of Ironcliff?"

"I have, although admittedly, not much. The vard there is a Dwarf named Grimdal, is he not?"

"No," said Kasri. "Not for some years now. The current ruler is Thalgrun Stormhammer."

"And what's he like?"

"He has his moments."

"You sound as if you know him well."

"I would hope so," said Herdwin. "He's her father."

Margel sat up. "Your father is the Vard of Ironcliff?"

"Yes, and Kasri is his designated successor, but don't tell anyone. We're trying to keep it secret for now."

"Not even Gelion?"

"Well, maybe him, but no one else, and you must swear him to secrecy."

"But I don't understand. Surely, we should celebrate your position?"

"No," said Kasri. "I'm here for Herdwin, not for my own self-glorification."

Margel's eyes flicked between her visitors. "Are you two forged?"

They both blushed.

"This is exciting," she continued. "How long has it been?"

"We're not forged," countered Kasri, "at least not yet. We came here to solve Herdwin's issues with the guild."

"Successor or not, they'll not see you. I hate to say it, Herdwin, but they have denounced you. It's forbidden for any member of the smiths guild to even mention your name. There's no coming back from something like that."

"They can't be serious? All that because he left them years ago?"

"I'm afraid it's more complicated than that. Herdwin dared to succeed without the guild's approval. That threatens their power within our people. Even now, there is talk amongst the younger generation that the guilds have become too oppressive. Every day, more speak of leaving Stonecastle to start a trade in one of the Human cities."

Herdwin grunted. "They'd be more than welcome. Trade thrives in Merceria, and they're always looking for more skilled artisans."

"Yes," added Kasri, "and there are no guilds, at least not that I've heard."

"There are some, but they don't control things to the extent they do here."

The door opened, admitting an armoured Dwarf. He removed his helmet, revealing a countenance not too dissimilar from Herdwin.

"Cousin Gelion!"

Margel stood, moving to hug her forge mate. "I must say, this is a surprise. I wasn't expecting you till late this afternoon?"

"One of my guards admitted to letting this rogue into the city." He nodded at Herdwin. "I knew he'd show up here sooner or later." His gaze fell on Kasri. "And I'm told he brought a female with him. That must be you."

"Kasri Ironheart," she replied. "From Ironcliff."

"Welcome to our home. I trust Margel has been looking after you?"

"She has indeed."

"Well then. Let me fetch an ale, and I'll join you." Gelion disappeared into the kitchen, only to quickly return tankard in hand. He placed his helmet on the floor and then took a seat beside his forge mate.

"How have things been?" asked Herdwin.

His cousin shrugged. "Walking the walls isn't the most exciting of duties, but every company has to take their turn."

"How many companies are here?" asked Kasri. "Or is asking that considered impertinent?"

"Not at all. There are ten full companies who take turns safeguarding the walls. If one of my guards hadn't mentioned your arrival, I would never have known you were here." He took a deep draught of his ale. "Speaking of which, why are you here?"

"He wants to settle things with the guild," said Margel.

"It's too late for that, I'm afraid."

"So I told him."

"It appears," said Herdwin, "I've wasted my time coming here."

"Don't say that," said Kasri. "There has to be something we can do?"

"There might be," said Gelion.

"Go on," said Herdwin. "I'm all ears."

His cousin glanced around the room, avoiding eye contact. "I'm not supposed to talk about this, but there has been some trouble to the east."

"So the guards indicated. Can you tell me the nature of the problem?"

"I'm afraid not, for to do so would break my oath of silence. However, your arrival here is most fortuitous. If I were you, I'd seek an audience with the vard. I'd be more than willing to arrange it if you like."

"To what end?"

"Let's just say your experience during the recent war might serve you well in this matter."

Herdwin shrugged. "I might as well. I came all this way. I'd hate to leave empty-handed."

"That's the spirit," said Kasri.

Gelion downed the last of his ale before he stood and picked up his helmet. "I'll head over there now and see when the vard is available."

"Available?" said Kasri. "Surely you mean if?"

"No. My cousin has done much for our ruler in the past. I don't believe there's any doubt he'll be granted an audience. The only unknown factor is when." Gelion donned his helmet and left.

"He'll get one," said Margel. "Just you wait and see. And as for when, I doubt you'll be waiting long."

"What makes you say that?" asked Kasri.

"Simple. These rumours of trouble to the east. There's a storm brewing, and I don't mean the kind that darkens the sky."

"How do you know that? Have you some sort of magic?"

"No, but I possess a bit of intuition, the same intuition that says you two are both going to be a big part of whatever it is."

That evening, Herdwin and Kasri were in separate rooms, appropriate, considering their non-forged status, yet he'd become so used to her company of late that he couldn't sleep.

For years, he'd been content to work away at his smithy in Wincaster, heedless of the distant guilds of Stonecastle, and he would've continued to do so had he not met Kasri. She let him dream of a shared future, but now it felt like it was all crumbling around him. Many male Dwarves never forged, for they outnumbered the females three to one, yet he now found himself suffering all the more for having his newfound hope shattered.

A soft knock at his door drew him from his brooding. "Come in," he called out. Kasri opened the door.

"What are you doing here?" he asked. "It isn't proper."

"I came to talk to you, nothing more."

"I'm afraid I'm not very good company right now."

"I thought not. That's why I'm here."

"To offer me solace? I don't think that will work."

"Then I shall go."

"No," said Herdwin. "Stay, please. I would feel better knowing you're here."

"Very well, but you must give up on this self-pity. You are Herdwin Steelarm, Dwarf commander and smith to the Queen of Merceria. Don't let the guild get the better of you."

"But don't you see? They are precisely the problem. Without their support, I'm an unsuitable candidate for you."

"That is not your decision to make."

"I'm only stating facts. You know as well as I do that a future vard cannot forge with someone with no guild membership."

Kasri stared at the floor. "So I've been told, but I refuse to believe the matter settled. Go to your friend, the vard, and perhaps he will provide the salvation we need."

EIGHT

The Lord of Stone

AUTUMN 966 MC

Vard Khazad sat upon his seat,
To render judgement fair.
Yet none could tell what danger lurked,
Or what might villains dare.

For farther east, a dark cloud spread,
The empire at its height.
Yet here in Dwarfhold, court of vards,
Did guildsmen curse and fight.

Khazad, the one-eyed Vard of Stonecastle, sat on his Throne, staring at the endless procession of guild representatives. It was a typical day, or at least would've been had it not been for news from the east.

The Dwarf before him blathered on about something,

but Khazad had long since given up paying the fellow any attention. Then, towards the back of the line, he noted movement. He stood, causing all within to fall silent.

"Herdwin Steelarm," he called out. "Come forward."

The room erupted into a cacophony of voices, for to the Dwarves, this was tantamount to scandal. One did not move to the front of the line; it simply wasn't done, particularly by someone the guilds had denounced. The newcomer stepped forward, joined by another who was a stranger to the court.

Vard Khazad looked down upon the pair of them. "What has brought you back to Stonecastle, Master Smith?" A hiss filled the audience chamber, for the vard conferred great honour with his manner of greeting.

"I come seeking a private audience, my vard."

"Do you, now? How impertinent of you. And who is this you bring before me?"

"Kasri Ironheart," he replied. "A skilled warrior from the fortress of Ironcliff."

"Is she also guildless?"

"No," said Kasri. "I'm a senior journeyman in the Warriors Guild of Ironcliff, ranked as a commander."

"Yet you travel in the company of this rogue. Why is that?"

"We're battle companions, Your Majesty, a friendship forged in war."

"Forged. An interesting turn of phrase for one of the mountain folk, wouldn't you say?"

"I've said it, and I will not take back my words."

Khazad smiled. "Nor would I expect you to. Tell me, how fares the Vard of Ironcliff?"

"He is well, Majesty, although of advanced years."

"Something which I am thoroughly familiar with. Would that our rulers could ascend to the Throne while still young, we would have so much more strength with which to act."

He lifted his eye patch and rubbed the eye socket beneath, giving him time to think. His attention then returned to his old acquaintance.

"Herdwin," he continued, "you've served us well in the recent war. You are to be commended on your bravery and your leadership. Your presence on the Nobles Council of Merceria has also given our people a voice there, something which greatly benefits us all"—his gaze swept the hall—"particularly the guilds."

"You honour me, my vard."

"Nonsense. It is us who should be honoured, merely by having you grace us with your presence." He used his index finger to indicate that Herdwin should advance. "I must publicly admonish you," he said, keeping his voice low. "Do not take offence at what comes next."

"Yes, Majesty."

Khazad sat up straight, raising his voice loud enough to be heard throughout the great hall. "However, though I welcome you here as a battle hero, it does not absolve you of your behaviour in turning your back on the most noble guild of smiths. You are, therefore, dismissed from this court as one forever banned from any guild of Stonecastle."

Even though the vard forewarned him, the words sliced through Herdwin like a knife, despair welling up despite his best efforts.

"Remove him from this hall," ordered the vard.

Guards moved forward, standing on either side of him. They led him out a side door, a disheartened Kasri following in their wake.

Behind the closed doors, the guards relaxed. "The rest of you return to your posts," said the sergeant. "You two, come with me. I'll take you to a room where you can await the vard in peace." He led them through a corridor.

"That's it?" said Kasri. "The great ruler of Stonecastle gives him a public reprimand and then expects him just to come and have a little chat?"

"Aye. That's about it."

Kasri shook her head. "This is all so confusing."

"He warned me," explained Herdwin. "It was for show, although, admittedly, it still stung."

"And what now?"

"Simple. We chat with the vard, just like you said."

"So that he can denounce you in private as well?"

"You mistake the vard's intentions," said the sergeant. "He has nothing but the highest regard for Master Herdwin. He did all that to appease the guilds. The scene will undoubtedly be the topic of conversation for days to come." He halted at a door. "Here we are. You may wait inside."

Herdwin and Kasri entered a small room, opulent in its decorations, with a few well-padded chairs sitting in a semi-circle before a lit fireplace.

"Quite the place," noted Kasri. "And these chairs look like they're made of shadowbark."

"They are," replied Herdwin. "The story goes they were

made from leftover wood from the construction of the city's great doors. We have a tradition of not wasting any resources."

"What's Vard Khazad like? You told me you worked under him in the miners guild but didn't give much of an idea about his personality."

"What would you like to know?"

"Anything?"

"Khazad has two personas: public and private. You saw his public face, playing the ever-dutiful servant to the guilds."

"And his private self?"

"A fellow dedicated to making life better for his subjects. He knows the guilds' weaknesses and plays to them. I've seen him outwit them time and again, only for them to be pleased with the results. I swear he has the luck of a dragon and the personality to go with it."

"I'm not sure what you mean. Are you saying he's personable?"

"He's always been good to me. He also realizes the benefits of staying on good terms with Merceria and knows I'm an important part of that, even if the guilds don't."

"And can he convince them to allow you membership?"

"I doubt it, but you never know. I'm sure he'll at least have a better idea of this trouble brewing in the east."

"The east can only mean one thing," said Kasri. "Halvaria."

"We don't know that for sure. Perhaps there's been trouble at the bridge? Maybe it's collapsed and in need of repair?"

"If that were the case, wouldn't they send engineers to repair it? And why put the garrison on alert?"

"Oh yes," said Herdwin. "I'd forgotten about that. I wasn't overly worried about the east until you brought that up."

"Sorry. I'm only trying to be realistic."

The door opened, admitting Khazad, the Lord of Stone. "Greetings," he began. "Have a seat, and make yourselves comfortable. It's not often I see an old friend."

"Or a new one, I hope," said Kasri.

"Ah, yes. Pleased to make your acquaintance, by the way."

"You honour me, Majesty."

"Bah, enough with the Majesty. We are amongst friends here. Call me Khazad." His good eye darted back and forth between his two guests. "Now, what is it you wanted to see me about?"

"Well," began Herdwin, "I don't know where to start. I came here hoping to get back into the guild's good graces."

"I'm afraid that rock has fallen, my friend, although I'm eager to know why. Has it something to do with Kasri here?"

"It does."

"I recognize that look. You two want to forge."

"We do, but there's a problem."

"Because she's the daughter of a vard?"

"You knew that?" asked Kasri.

"Of course. Did you honestly believe I wouldn't recognize your name? Herdwin's reports told me all about you."

"Oh yes," replied the smith. "Of course, I should've realized that."

"Has this to do with your lack of standing amongst our people?"

"Yes," said Herdwin.

"I'm afraid there is little I can do regarding the guilds, but I might be able to raise your status some, if that's any help. It would definitely nudge you in the right direction." He walked over to a nearby table and poured some ale.

Kasri moved towards him. "Have you no servants, Majesty?"

"I am quite capable of pouring ale all by myself. This may surprise you, but I wasn't always a vard. I used to work for a living." He held out a tankard. "Here, take this." He poured another.

"You mentioned status?" said Herdwin. "What did you mean by that?"

"Merely that an opportunity may have presented itself. Your arrival here comes at a most fortunate time, at least from my point of view."

"Why? What's happened?"

"It's the east," said the Lord of Stone. "One of the beacons is unresponsive."

"I'm not sure I understand," said Kasri.

"We have beacons sitting astride the path to the east and west. Well, I say beacon, but the reality is they're towers with a massive bowl above them, holding a signal fire, which we only light when danger threatens."

"And a beacon's been lit?"

"No, precisely the opposite. Every evening at midnight, each tower will, in turn, raise a lantern, signalling all's well. Unfortunately, we received word the tower farthest east has failed to respond for two nights straight."

"Surely you sent warriors to investigate?" asked Kasri.

"We're preparing to, but we only just received the news. You see, one missed night is not a cause for worry, but two? Well, that's tempting fate, don't you think?" He held out another tankard. "This one's for you, Herdwin."

"You want us to investigate?" said Kasri.

"You know, I didn't consider that."

"Liar," said Herdwin. "That's the only reason you agreed to speak to us, isn't it?"

"All right. I confess I hoped you'd volunteer. After all, I can't very well command you to do anything, not with you being banned from guild membership."

"What does that mean, exactly?" asked Kasri. "Is he also banned from the city limits?"

"No," replied the vard. "The fact is it's almost entirely ceremonial in nature. Of course, it prevents you from joining any other guild in Stonecastle, but then again, you care little about that, or at least you did the last time I saw you. However, I think Kasri might have changed your mind on such things." Having finished pouring his own drink, he took a sip. "I must say you two make a fitting couple. Have you made an official announcement?"

"No. My father forbade me to forge with Herdwin until the smiths guild accepts him."

The vard wandered over, collapsing into a chair, then pulled off his boots and wiggled his toes. "The blasted boot-makers guild is getting away with shoddy work these days. My feet have never been so sore."

"Have you heard of Halvaria?" asked Kasri.

"No," said Khazad. "Can't say I have. Why? Who are they?"

"This is only speculation, but I suspect they may be the threat lying to the east. At least they are in Ironcliff."

"Tell me more about them."

"They are a Human empire, and from what we've seen, they don't much like non-Humans."

"That doesn't sound good."

"It's not. We've had several run-ins with them of late, although not an outright invasion. It's almost as if they're assessing our strength."

"Do you need assistance?"

"We allied ourselves with Merceria," replied Kasri.

"And will that be enough?"

"It's too early to tell, but if they are to the east of Stonecastle, it makes them an even larger threat."

Khazad took another sip of his ale, swishing it around his mouth before swallowing. "Have you any information on their weapons or armour?"

"Those warriors we've seen fall into two categories. You might classify them as light foot and heavy."

"Any archers?"

"Aye," she replied, "though I doubt their weapons would outdistance our arbalesters. As to numbers or organization, we possess little knowledge. For all we know, there may be more to the army of this realm. They also worship a god-emperor."

"Who is?"

"We have no idea, merely that they revere him as a deity."

"Has your father made any attempts at formal nego-
tiations?"

"He has, on several occasions. Most returned empty-
handed, but we fear they executed those who did not
return."

Khazad took a sip of his ale. "And if it is the Halvarians
probing from the east?"

"Then you should send an expedition to deal them a
blow from which they will never recover."

"That would be difficult. The eastern approaches to
Stonecastle are treacherous, certainly not the type of terrain
from which to launch an attack."

"But easy to defend?"

"Precisely. So, a counterattack in force is not something
we can consider, not if we want a half-decent chance of
success, and I'll not throw the lives of our warriors away
recklessly."

"These towers," said Kasri. "How big are they?"

"Large enough to house half a dozen warriors. Their task
is to watch the east and light the signal fire if danger
threatens."

"And if they're attacked?"

"They are to hold out for as long as possible. To that end,
we built the towers to withstand a siege."

"That would seem to indicate it's unlikely one was
captured. Could it have fallen to some calamity? Say, sickness, for example?"

"I hadn't considered that as an option. They're an
isolated garrison. Where would the sickness come from?"

"I assume you rotate the garrison?" she asked.

"Of course. Ah, I see what you're getting at. One of them likely took the illness with them when they reported for duty. I suppose it's a distinct possibility, but I'd be reluctant to send others on a rescue mission if that were the case. We might infect the entire city."

"Then let us go," said Herdwin. "If we find anything dangerous, we'll light the signal fire."

"And if there is sickness there?"

"Then we'll raise a red flag," offered Kasri.

Herdwin chuckled. "In Merceria, the red flag signifies rebellion."

"Then so be it," said Khazad. "But I shall send warriors to follow in your wake. There's still the possibility these Halvarians you spoke of are probing our defences. Do you believe your cousin would be up to the task?"

"Yes."

"Good, then the matter is settled. Have you armour?"

"Aye," said Kasri. "Though I wish I'd brought my plate instead of my mail. Still, it has served me well enough in the past—it will do so again."

"If you need anything else, feel free to contact me. Now, I must go. Good luck, and may Gundar watch over you."

That afternoon, the two of them were sitting in the Iron Ingot, a local tavern full of boisterous Dwarves, making conversation difficult, though not impossible.

"Well?" said Kasri. "What's on your mind?"

"I was thinking about that signal tower."

"And?"

"The more I do," said Herdwin, "the more I become convinced some calamity has befallen them, and I don't mean a sickness."

"Why ever not? People do get sick from time to time."

"Yes, but all at once and fast enough that they couldn't somehow signal for help? They could've at least hoisted a lantern, indicating something was wrong."

"You believe it's the Humans to the east," said Kasri.

"I do, though I'm not ready to identify them as Halvarians. It could just be another Human kingdom attempting to stretch its borders. I'm told it's a common enough occurrence amongst their people. What do you think?"

"What you say sounds reasonable. Something's definitely brewing in the east."

"So you think this tower is only the beginning?"

"I do, and it bodes ill for both our homes."

"My home is in Wincaster," said Herdwin.

"I understand that, but you're allied with Stonecastle, and that alliance goes both ways. Merceria would come to its aid if they came under attack."

"I imagine there'll be more than one Human noble who objects to that."

"True," said Kasri, "but the queen will honour the pledge, and where she leads, others follow. The question is whether it'll be enough."

"They've managed worse."

"We don't know that. The fact is we know next to nothing about this threat. How large is their army? What's their quality? We don't even know how big their empire is."

"We need to learn more," said Herdwin. "Were we back

in Merceria, I would suggest the Orcs use their magic to contact their cousins in the east. At the very least, they may have heard of these people."

"An excellent idea, one we should follow up with on our return, but we must deal with the here and now. How far away is this tower?"

"There are at least two of them to the east. I'm sure Gelion can tell us more."

"And it's the most eastward one they're worried about?"

"It is. That means another trip through mountain passes, and this time of year, it'll be cold. Let's hope winter doesn't come early, or we may find ourselves trudging through the snow."

NINE

The Mission

AUTUMN 966 MC

We have ourselves a problem,
Said the king, and it is great.
We need a pair of heroes,
To go investigate.

Then let us go, said Herdwin brave,
With Kasri at his side.
And we shall find what's gone amiss,
And rescue Dwarven pride.

"Pass the sausages," said Herdwin.

"You're lucky," said Margel, handing him the plate. "Those are rare in these parts."

"He's developed a taste for them," explained Kasri. "I understand they're a favourite of the Mercerian marshal."

"They are," added Herdwin. "And the queen serves him only the best."

"And these?"

"They're quite passable, in their own way, but goat sausage is something of an acquired taste. Now, these"—he stabbed a potato—"these are a gift from the Gods. How do you get them so juicy?"

Margel laughed. "I don't think I've ever heard a potato described as juicy before. It's the lard I use to coat them before cooking."

"I'll have to try that back home. I'm sure Gerald would like it. What do you think, Kasri?"

"They're quite nice." She was about to say more when a knock at the door interrupted the conversation.

"Who can that be this early in the morning?" asked Margel.

"There's only one way to find out," said Gelion. He rushed to the door to see a Dwarf warrior waiting, one of the king's personal guards.

"Captain Gelion, is Master Herdwin here? I bear a message from the Lord of Stone."

"He is. Come in."

The warrior stepped into the room, doffing his helmet and nodding at Margel. "My apologies for the interruption, mistress." He pulled a scroll case from his belt. "This is for you, Master Herdwin."

Herdwin took the scroll case, then broke the seal and removed the cap. Inside rested a single page, which he removed and read while everyone else waited with bated breath.

"Thank you, Sergeant," said Herdwin. "You may return to His Majesty and inform him we will begin at once."

He held off until the visitor left before turning to face the others. "It appears there's been a development."

"Of what nature?" said Kasri.

"The beacon has been lit. We are now under attack."

"Then, as you said, we must be on our way."

"We?" said Gelion. "Surely you don't mean to go yourself, Kasri? That would be unconscionable?"

"I am a warrior."

"Yes, but you're also a female."

"What of it? We fight the same as you do."

"In battle, true, but we're talking about going into the unknown. That's much more dangerous."

Kasri reddened. "How dare you speak thus to me! I am the commander of the Hearth Guard of Ironcliff. I do not shrink at the thought of danger."

Gelion opened his mouth, but Margel placed her hand on his forearm, causing him to pause. "She is the daughter of a vard," she said. "You have no say over her actions."

Gelion stared with a gaping mouth. "What?"

"She speaks the truth," said Kasri. "I am Kasri Ironheart, wielder of Stormhammer, leader of the Hearth Guard, successor to Thalgrun, Vard of Ironcliff, and a dragon rider, perhaps even the only one in all the known lands."

"And you chose Herdwin?"

Margel elbowed him. "Don't be rude."

"I'm not," he replied, "but Herdwin has no standing in the guilds. How, then, can he forge with a future vard?"

"That," said Kasri, "is not something you need concern yourself with."

"On another note," said Herdwin, "you're ordered to assemble your company."

"To accompany you?" asked Gelion.

"More or less. You'll follow at a respectful distance."

"What does that mean?"

"Far enough that we can approach the tower without fear of you being seen, but close enough you can move up and assist should a fight develop."

"I can do that."

"Good. Now tell us more about these towers."

"There are four to the east, and they all follow the same design. Each is square at its base with three floors. The guard room, with a hearth to keep it warm, is located on the ground level. The second floor contains the sleeping quarters, while the third has the armoury and lots of wood to fire up the beacon."

"How does the beacon work?" asked Kasri.

"It's essentially a large metal bowl with holes along the bottom for water to drain. You can access it through a ladder on the top floor."

"Is the beacon always ready to go?"

"It is, but the weather often plays havoc with it. Typically, they would pile new wood on the old before lighting it."

"And if it's raining?"

"It's more likely to snow, but they stock oil to help with combustion. There's also a long pole on the corner of the roof for raising signal lanterns."

"And the tower only houses six warriors at a time?"

"That's correct. They used to house twenty-four, but the guilds complained about the cost."

"And the doors?"

"Reinforced with iron bands and barred from the inside. They can use the windows on the second and third floors to shoot arbalest bolts."

"All this is interesting," said Herdwin, "but how long could a garrison hold out if attacked?"

"There are many things to consider," said Gelion, "but assuming their enemy didn't have siege engines—likely weeks. They'd certainly have enough food."

"Wouldn't an attack be seen from the next tower?"

"No. From that distance, they can only see the fires or the lanterns with any certainty."

"Let's hope the garrison is holed up inside," said Kasri. "I shouldn't like to need to assault the place."

"We may have no choice," said Herdwin.

"Actually," said Gelion, "we do. The alternative would be to abandon it and move back across Kharzun's Folly."

"That's the bridge Taldur spoke of, isn't it? Perhaps it wasn't such a far-fetched idea after all."

"Even a bridge can't be held forever," said Kasri.

"True, but it would buy us time."

"To do what?"

"That," said Herdwin, "I'm still working on. In any case, we need to concentrate on finding out who's attacking. I know you think it's Halvaria, but we must make sure."

"Ironcliff is close to five hundred miles away," said Gelion. "Surely this Halvaria isn't that big?"

"It's not that big when you think about it. Merceria is about five hundred miles from east to west, and they say Norland is even larger."

"Yes, but they're sparsely populated."

"How do we know the same isn't true of Halvaria?"

"You make a good point, Cousin, but let's hope it's not them. I don't much like the idea of going up against a kingdom that big."

"When will you leave?" asked Margel.

"Right away," said Herdwin. "We've some distance to cover before nightfall."

"How far is it?" asked Kasri.

"According to this letter, the towers are a day apart. Mind you, it's not a straight distance. Much of the path folds back on itself as it climbs higher into the mountains."

Margel rose. "I'll fetch you some warm cloaks to keep the chill at bay. Gelion, you'd best assemble your warriors."

"Very well," answered her forge mate. "I shall see you two on the road."

Herdwin and Kasri stepped through the gate to spot a lone figure waiting for them.

"Greetings," said Delsaran.

"What are you doing here?" asked Kasri.

"I convinced the king that I should accompany you."

"To what end?"

"Why, to tell of your exploits. This is a momentous time in the history of Stonecastle. I must record your deeds for posterity."

"Bah," said Herdwin. "We'll likely find the garrison has merely passed out after drinking too much. I doubt that would make an interesting song."

"Then the only thing wasted would be my time," the Elf persisted. "And even if there is nothing of interest, I have yet to finish your story."

"My story? What nonsense is that?"

"Lord Arandil told me of your exploits in the recent Mercerian war. Why, my friend, you are the hero of Galburn's Ridge!"

"Don't be daft. Prince Alric's men stormed the keep, along with those of Sir Preston."

"Yet you survived the first aborted attempt."

"I'd hardly call that valiant, more like too stubborn to die."

"There is a lot to be said for being stubborn. Particularly in this case, but that is only one example of your heroics. And Kasri has not escaped my notice, for I also learned of her accomplishments."

"I'd warrant the songs of bards are seldom based on fact," said Herdwin. "Rather, they glorify the mundane."

"Well, we do need to keep people entertained after all."

"Have you ever drawn that sword of yours?"

"No," replied Delsaran. "And, just to be clear, I am only here as an observer. When the going gets difficult, I shall be but a distant bystander, recording events as they happen. However, should either of you die in this endeavour, I will immortalize your tale. Is there any particular epithet you would like to be remembered by?"

"What do you mean?"

"Well, would you want to be known as Herdwin the Brave, for example? Or how about Herdwin Steelarm, the hero of something or other?"

Herdwin chuckled. "The hero of something or other?"

"I will come up with a more suitable title for you. Consider it a work in progress."

"And me?" said Kasri.

"That's easy. You are Kasri, the Dragon Rider. Herdwin needs something a little more grandiose than master smith."

"That's grand enough for me," she said.

"Ah, the voice of true love. How touching. I shall make sure to include that in my epic tale."

"I thought it was a song?"

"It is," defended the Elf, "but it still tells a story. In my experience, songs are much easier to remember than mere tales, and the accompanying music plays to the heart."

"Plays to the heart?"

"Yes, sets the mood. Why, with the strum of a lute, I can make the audience feel happy or sad."

"You don't have a lute," said Herdwin.

"Not with me, no, but I have several back home."

"Several?" said Kasri. "Why?"

"I have accumulated a collection of them. I am, after all, an Elf, which means I have lived a great many years compared to you two."

"Yet this is the first time you've left home?"

"Only in the sense of leaving the Darkwood. I travel from town to town, within the woods, of course." He suddenly went quiet, his face turning red. "I think I said too much."

"Very well," said Herdwin. "You may accompany us, but we must be on our way if we want to reach the first tower by nightfall. I trust you remembered to bring food this time?"

"I did."

"Good. Now come along. We've no time to waste."

Stonecastle backed onto one of many mountains in this range. As they journeyed, the path veered both north and south, twisting as it made its way up and down the many slopes and cliffs. They paused at noon, the gathering clouds obstructing their view of the sun.

"How about Herdwin the Heroic?" asked Delsaran.

"I've never been one to seek glory," replied the smith.

"Yet you led the Army of Stonecastle?"

"That was to help my friends. Merceria is my home now, not that wretched place back there."

"You hate your own people that much?"

"I'm all for tradition," said Herdwin, "but Stonecastle is like a wall of stone, immovable and resolute, unable to change with the rest of the land. Merceria, on the other hand, is a land of opportunity, where a person can make a living by the sweat of their own labours, not the whims of an ancient system of guilds."

"Are you a rebel, then?"

"Aye, I suppose I am. After all, I supported the usurper during the Mercerian Civil War."

"Yet Mistress Kasri represents that same system of guilds, does she not?"

"What are you getting at?"

"I am merely curious how you two became such close friends?"

"We fought side by side," explained Kasri. "Battle brings people together in ways you wouldn't understand."

"Then explain it to me."

"I can't speak for all, but I believe battle brings out the most savage parts of us. At that moment, you get caught up in the fight, the blood pumping through you so fast you can feel your heart pounding in your chest. It gives you a sense of euphoria. The same feeling as when someone you care about is nearby." She reached out, putting her hand on Herdwin's knee.

"I see," said the Elf. "Does it make you fight any differently?"

"Yes. It makes you more cautious, less willing to take risks."

"Are you saying it makes you less effective as a warrior?"

"No, quite the reverse. With no one in their life, a warrior feels impervious to harm. So much so that they take significant risks in battle. Sometimes, that can work in your favour, but it often leads to unnecessary death."

"And when you have someone?"

"You tend to examine the situation in greater detail, look for options other than simply charging ahead at full speed. It's a characteristic of a skilled commander."

"I see," said Delsaran. "And how many great commanders have you met?"

"Lots. Most of them Mercerian, but I know a Dwarf who fits that description quite nicely." She smiled at Herdwin.

"Though, come to think of it, I suppose he's a Mercerian as well."

"But that is not where he was born."

"Nor were many people who now serve the Queen of Merceria. Belonging isn't limited by your place of birth—it's a state of mind."

"Perhaps I should call you Kasri the Philosopher?"

"I would take that as a compliment."

"All this is well and good," said Herdwin, "but if we wait here any longer, Gelion and his warriors will catch up."

"And is that a bad thing?" asked Delsaran.

"It is when we've got a job to do. Now, come. Lift that sorry rear end of yours off the ground, and let's get moving."

The road narrowed as they continued, forcing them to walk single file at some points, but the cliffs were the worst, for the trail was so thin there, they had to press their backs against the rock to avoid plummeting to their deaths.

Delsaran, unwisely choosing to look down, was soon overcome with a sense of vertigo. He leaned back against the cliff face, his eyes closed, muttering a silent prayer to Tauril.

Herdwin soon appeared at his side. "Are you all right?"

The Elf shook his head. "Do you not fear the drop, Master Dwarf?"

"Of course not."

"I wish I had your courage."

"It's not courage but practicality."

Delsaran opened his eyes. "I am afraid you must explain that to me."

"Great heights don't kill."

"Yes, they do!"

"No. It's only the sudden stop at the bottom. The fact of the matter is there's no better way to die."

"How can you possibly say that?"

"Simple. Death comes the instant your body strikes the ground. From a height like this, it would be painless."

"Unless you strike the cliff on your way down."

"Yes. I suppose there is that," said Herdwin. "Look, you lived in the Darkwood. Surely you've fallen out of a tree before?"

"I have."

"Then think of this cliff as just a gigantic tree."

"That hardly helps."

"Then put such thoughts aside. Concentrate on the epic tale this will make. Instead of merely telling it, you're a part of it all. The great Delsaran, risking his very existence to bring a story to life."

"Your argument is compelling. Very well, let us continue on this most noble of quests." Delsaran took a deep breath, trying to gather his courage. "Before we do, could you answer a question?"

"If I can."

"Why is this ledge so narrow? My understanding is that the eastern approaches were meant to facilitate trade?"

"And so they were," said Herdwin, "but that trade never materialized, and over the centuries, the wind and rain have taken their toll."

"But a path such as this is treacherous."

"Not to a Dwarf, though I must admit it could stand to be widened a bit. Perhaps I'll suggest it to the king upon our return."

"You mean the vard?"

"Ah," said Herdwin. "I see you finally adopted some of our terms. We'll make an ambassador out of you yet."

"I am a bard."

"For now, but in the fullness of time, who can say where your travels might take you? Grasp my hand, and I will guide you past this ledge."

Delsaran inched along, his back pressed tightly against the cliff face. He craned his neck, keeping his eyes fastened firmly on Herdwin, permitting him to forget the drop, at least for the present. The ledge soon widened, allowing them to walk with ease.

"Are there any more ledges like that?" asked Delsaran.

"I haven't a clue."

TEN

The Beacon

AUTUMN 966 MC

Unto a beacon they did go,
A tower made of stone.
Yet there within stood soldiers firm,
Who took it as their own.

And so they fought the empire's might,
This couple from the west.
And axe and hammer struck down all,
As heroes gave their best.

I t took them five days to reach their destination, which included a day spent within a tower as a violent storm raged along the mountain trails. The garrisons at each stop were most welcoming, particularly the third, as they'd reported the trouble in the first place.

Early the following day, Herdwin and Kasri climbed to the top of the tower, the better to get a look at their destination.

"The fire is out," said Kasri, "but I have no idea if that bodes ill or well."

"There is some sort of activity," Herdwin replied. "Although I can't make out any details."

The hatch opened, revealing the grey countenance of Delsaran.

"You surprise me," said Kasri. "I didn't think you liked heights."

"Nor do I," replied the Elf, "but I came to find out what the two of you were looking at."

"Your arrival is most fortuitous." She pointed eastward. "Our destination lies over yonder. I'm told that Elves' vision is superior to the mountain folk. What do you see?"

Delsaran steadied himself against the huge metal bowl holding the signal fire. "There is movement over there," he said. "Although it does not appear to be Dwarves."

"Are you sure?"

"Indeed. Note how they walk—they must be Humans, if I am not mistaken."

"So," said Kasri, "it's Halvaria, then?"

"We don't know that," said Herdwin, "and likely won't till we get a closer look. Your people met them before. Is there anything distinctive about them?"

"The few warriors we've encountered bore a surcoat emblazoned with a dragon intertwined around a tree. At least that's how our scouts interpreted it. Of course, we don't know if that was the mark of a local lord or their emperor."

"I see horses," called out Delsaran.

"Where?"

"Tethered right behind the tower, likely to keep them out of sight."

"The thing I want to know is where have the Dwarves gone?"

"I suspect they're dead," said Herdwin. "Although, I suppose it's feasible they might've been taken prisoner. Either way, we won't know more until we get closer. How many do you see, Delsaran?"

"Outside? Just three, and only the briefest of views of the horses, really no more than the occasional swish of a tail, or I could give you a better description."

"And their armour?"

"Bad news, I am afraid. They appear to be wearing mail, and at least one has a breastplate, similar to what I believe they use in Merceria."

"Thank Gundar, it's not full plate," said Kasri. "If there are three outside, there are likely to be more within. The question, of course, is how many? I suggest we get as close as possible. Any way of approaching from the other side?"

"No," said Herdwin. "The terrain won't allow it. We must cross a massive gorge just to get there."

"Let me guess, Kharzun's Folly?"

"Yes. Unfortunately, you can't see it from here. That ridge over yonder blocks its view. The road snakes around to the south and then doubles back to cross over."

"I thought you'd never been here?" said Delsaran.

"I haven't, but the tower captain here described it to me."

"How do we proceed?"

"If we can get close enough," said Kasri, "we might be able to learn a thing or two about what they've got planned."

"Wait," said Delsaran. "If these Humans control the tower, then who lit the fire?"

"I hadn't considered that," said Herdwin. "But now you mention it, it could only be the Halvarians."

"Why would they send a warning?"

"Likely to lure us in. How better to test our strength than by alerting us to danger?"

"Yes," agreed Delsaran, "but that would make it difficult to press their attack, would it not?"

"I doubt this is a full-scale invasion, more likely a testing of our defences."

"Or our resolve," added Kasri. "In either case, we can't let the challenge go unanswered, or they'll return in greater numbers."

"Why now, I wonder?"

Kasri smiled. "Perhaps a prisoner or two might shed light on their motives."

"A good idea. Delsaran, can you use a bow?"

"Why is it everyone thinks all Elves can use a bow? Do all Dwarves use axes?"

"Yes," said Kasri. "Although some prefer the hammer or even the sword."

"Answer the question," said Herdwin. "Can you use a bow or not?"

"I possess a passing familiarity with them," replied the Elf, "but it matters not. I did not bring one."

"Ah, but we did. At least, we have an arbalest."

"You do?"

"Yes, in the armoury in the tower. Look, I'm not expecting you to be an expert with it, but even a stray bolt or two might help dissuade the enemy from rushing that bridge."

"The bridge? You mean Kharzun's Folly? Surely, you have no intentions of crossing it?"

"How else will we reach our target?"

"Don't worry," said Kasri. "I believe I know what he has in mind, and you get to stay at the safe end."

"And which end is the safe one?"

"The one closest to here," said Herdwin. "Now, are you willing to help and become part of the legend or not?"

"Yes, but I would feel braver if I could get off the top of this tower."

"In that case, let's go below and see what else we might find in the armoury."

By the time they reached the gorge, the sun was well past its zenith. The bridge, however, still lay some fifty feet below, for the distance across the top was far too great for even Dwarven engineering to master. The road continued against the cliffside, down to an outcropping of rock used as the base of the bridge.

The impressive stone structure spanned a gap rivalling the best range a skilled archer might manage with any accuracy. The arched centre rose nearly two stories above either end without any support beneath.

Herdwin stood on one side of the bridge, leaning over the edge, staring down into the sheer drop, the distance impossible to calculate with the mist. Even so, he heard running water far below as a mountain stream rushed through the gap.

"It is quite the marvel," said Kasri. "How long did it take to make, I wonder?"

"Years," the smith replied. "Although I don't know the exact count. Your guess is as good as mine as to how they built it."

"Why the arch in the middle?"

"It likely has something to do with the distance involved. The bulk of the structure resembles an arch bridge, with the weight born by the cliffs on either side, but that middle part looks like an afterthought as if the design hadn't been large enough to span the gap."

"I thought you knew nothing about its construction?"

"I don't, at least not any more than the next Dwarf. Still, it's an amazing sight to see in person."

"Earth Magic," said Kasri.

"I beg your pardon?"

"I've seen the kind of work Agramath can do. It wouldn't surprise me if a master of rock and stone were involved here."

"They don't have such folk in Stonecastle," replied Herdwin. "Admittedly, my knowledge of such things is a little outdated. However, that doesn't mean they lacked them in the past. I think you've got the right of it when you say mages were involved with this bridge. Tell me, Delsaran, do you have any engineering to rival this back in the Darkwood?"

"Certainly not on this scale," replied the Elf, "though we have some long suspension bridges. We use them to traverse the Darkwood at great speed."

"Your rivers are that wide?"

"No, but we travel from treetop to treetop. It allows us to watch what happens below with little chance of discovery."

"Shall we cross?" asked Kasri.

"Most certainly," said Herdwin. "What of you, Delsaran? Care to join us?"

"I thought you wanted me on this side?"

"Eventually, but we must find out what we're dealing with first."

"Very well," said the Elf, "but I intend to come back here at the first sign of trouble."

"Agreed."

When they started, the bridge was wide enough for ten warriors to stand side by side, with a railing to keep them safe, but it narrowed as they advanced until it was barely wide enough for two. Near the centre, a second bridge had been built upon the first, this one narrower still, continuing for nearly thirty paces to meet the other side.

"Wait here," said Herdwin.

He advanced, climbing the smaller section to the very centre, where he halted and looked all around. The wind was quite pronounced, and the lack of railing on this part forced him to consider why they'd built it in such a fashion. On a hunch, he laid flat, peering over the edge.

Beneath the centre bridge were cut stones and, at their peak, a very prominent keystone set with Dwarven runes. He carefully got to his feet, quickly returning to his companions.

"Well?" said Kasri. "Learn anything interesting?"

"I did, indeed. A keystone holds that centre span together. Destroy it, and I suspect the entire bridge will collapse, or at least that middle section."

"So, do we destroy it now?" asked Delsaran.

"No. We've yet to determine the fate of those who defended the fourth tower. We must proceed with caution, but it will likely be dangerous. I'd like you to remain here, Delsaran."

"To what end?"

"Gelion should soon arrive with his warriors. Ask him to line his arbalesters along this side of this gorge to oppose any who might try to cross."

"And you?"

"Kasri and I will get as close as possible to these Humans and see what we can discover."

"Be careful, my friend. I should very much like you to live long enough to hear my ballad of your heroics."

Herdwin laughed. "I can't make any guarantees, but I'll do my best."

"As will I," added Kasri. "How much farther is the tower, do you reckon?"

"Once we cross the gorge, we need only climb that rise, and then it should be within sight."

"Then let's get going while we still have an afternoon to act."

They walked across slowly, keeping their eyes glued to the other side of the gorge. There was always the chance their enemy might be watching the bridge, but there were no signs of alarm if such were the case. Soon, they were both on solid mountain footing once more.

"Should we draw weapons?" asked Kasri.

"Probably a good idea." Herdwin pulled the axe from his belt but left his shield on his back.

Kasri unslung her own shield, aware of her lack of heavy armour. Stormhammer, too, was out and ready for use as they neared the top of the rise. They both crouched, staring at the tower standing off in the distance. From this angle, they could see some horses tied off behind the tower.

"Only six," said Kasri, her voice low. "Not bad odds, if I do say so myself. Shall we charge now, or try to take them by surprise?"

"Surprise would be better—less opportunity of one of them getting away on horseback and raising the alarm."

"We should circle around to the right. There's a boulder over there that would make the ideal cover."

"You take the lead; I'll be right behind you."

Kasri stayed crouched while she moved towards the large boulder. She was halfway there when a guard called out. She turned to face the Humans, ready to hurl a bolt of lightning their way, but whoever shouted was only talking to one of his companions. Relieved, she quickly completed her trip.

Upon seeing her freeze, Herdwin turned his attention to

the tower. His first thought was someone had spied them from atop the structure, but to his surprise, there was no one up there. It seemed a significant thing to ignore, but then he remembered it would reveal their presence to tower number three. He noticed Kasri waving him over, so he crossed the gap, sliding in beside her.

They were close now, less than thirty paces from the horses, close enough to hear what might transpire between these Humans, but as luck would have it, the foreign invaders remained silent.

Kasri tapped his shield, reminding him to remove it from his back. He nodded, taking it in hand, ready to begin the assault.

"Straight for the door," he whispered, "but stay close. We may need to fight back to back."

"Agreed."

They advanced quietly, their unspoken agreement to rush at the first sign of discovery. Halfway to the target, Herdwin's foot kicked a stone, drawing the attention of one of the Humans. The fellow turned, revealing a tunic emblazoned with the distinctive dragon wrapped around a tree.

Herdwin charged forward, his axe swinging even as the poor fool attempted to draw his sword. The man fell under the onslaught of Herdwin's attack as Kasri let loose with a bolt of lightning, taking another in the chest.

Witnessing the sudden attack, a third man ran for the door. Dwarves are not known as the fastest runners, but the Halvarian had a greater distance to cross, so Kasri beat him, rushing in before anyone closed the door. Herdwin stopped behind her, turning to intercept the runner, smashing out with his shield, and driving the fellow to the ground. A quick axe swing finished him off, and then the smith turned his attention to the tower.

Kasri entered the main floor, where two startled individuals sat at a table. One fell from his chair in his rush to get to his feet while the other had the presence of mind to hurl a knife her way. She stopped to block the feeble attack, giving the villain a chance to back up and draw his sword.

Kasri let loose with another bolt of lightning only to instantly regret it, for the thunderclap echoed off the walls, the reverberations ringing in her ears. Her blast struck the man on the floor, silencing him, but his companion, now clutching his head, retreated, keeping his back to the hearth. Stepping forward, she smashed him with the hammer, but he deflected the blow and even counterattacked, his weapon faster and nimbler than hers.

Something hit her from behind, and she wheeled around as a sword scraped along her arm. Her Dwarven chain stopped the blow, but now enemies surrounded her.

Herdwin, spotting the threat, barrelled right into the hapless fool behind her, knocking him over. A quick follow-up attack to the man's arm sent his foe's weapon flying, followed by a cry of, "Mercy!"

Kasri, meanwhile, advanced on the last of them. "Give up," she demanded.

"I surrender." He lowered his sword before tossing it to the floor.

Herdwin prodded his prisoner to sit at the table, then pulled the surcoat from the man's shoulders, tossing the material to Kasri. "Here. Tear this up and then use it to bind your fellow's arms while I see to this one's wound."

"You heard him," she said. "Turn around."

It didn't take long to tie his hands behind his back before righting the chair and sitting him at the table.

Herdwin, having bound the injured man, now forced him to sit. "Time for some answers," he said. "Where are the Dwarves who occupied this tower?"

"Dead," replied the injured man. "We caught them by surprise."

"You killed them all?"

"No, not at first. Two died in the initial attack, two more a little later, after succumbing to their wounds."

"And the other two?"

"They refused to speak to us, despite the best efforts of our truthseeker."

"Where are the bodies?" asked Kasri.

"We tossed them into the gorge."

"And where is this truthseeker you speak of?"

"He left to join the others."

"What others?" said Herdwin.

"Why, the army, of course. You don't think we came here with only half a dozen men?"

"Why are you telling us all this? Aren't you worried your commander will be upset with you revealing your plans?"

"Of course not. None can withstand the army of the god-emperor."

"Then please tell me," said Kasri. "Why didn't you place a watch on the bridge?"

"We wanted to lure more of you to cross, the better to learn about your people, and it worked."

"That's why you lit the signal fire," said Herdwin.

The prisoner relaxed. "Would you like to surrender now, or fight it out when the others come?"

Kasri ran to the door, quickly closing it and throwing down the drop bar. Even as the wooden timber fell into place, they heard the distinctive sound of horseshoes on the roadway.

"Give yourself over to the emperor's army, and we will grant you a quick death."

"A quick death, is it?" said Kasri. "Let me think about that for a moment. Hmmm, that would be a definite no. You, Herdwin?"

"That's a pretty bold statement for someone who's tied up, but I'm with Kasri on this one."

"Then you both shall die," said the prisoner.

ELEVEN

Trapped

AUTUMN 966 MC

The enemy did come in droves,
And trapped our two asunder.
While empire troops prepared to march,
To Dwarven home to plunder.

Yet through the night our heroes fought,
To gain the upper hand.
That they would buy some time for Dwarves,
To save their cherished land.

"Now you're trapped," said the prisoner. "But if you give up and tell us what we want to know, we'll spare your lives."

"So that's it?" said Herdwin. "I didn't come all this way only to surrender."

"Your defeat is inevitable. No one can resist the power of the emperor."

"This seems to be a theme with you. Have you never lost a battle?"

"Never."

"That's easy enough to explain," said Kasri. "They likely don't talk of such things; it would be bad for morale."

"What is your name?" asked Herdwin.

"I am called Darfal."

"And you're, what? One of Halvaria's elite warriors?"

"Me? No. I'm merely a provincial."

"Meaning?"

"They recruited me from a province liberated by the emperor's warriors."

"You mean conquered," said Herdwin.

The prisoner merely shrugged. "Call it what you want, but the land has prospered since they absorbed us."

"Absorbed?" said Kasri. "That hardly sounds like it was voluntary."

"Some opposed it, but that is always the way when progress is involved."

"And what happened to those who disagreed with the change in leadership?"

"They were sent away to re-evaluate their purpose in life."

"And this didn't strike you as odd?"

"They reward those of us who embrace the empire."

"By sending you to the middle of a mountain range to die?"

"I am happy to give my life for the glorification of the

emperor."

"And this emperor," said Herdwin. "Has he ever spoken to you?"

"Only through his faithful, the seekers of truth."

"Like the one who ran away?"

"He didn't run," said Darfal. "As I told you earlier, he returned to the rest of the expedition."

"And just how big is this expedition you speak of?"

"It numbers in the hundreds."

"How many hundreds?"

"Three, maybe four. More than enough to take care of you two."

"You expect us to believe your masters would send that many men just to scout a narrow path?"

"I expect nothing; I merely tell the truth. For years, rumours told of a trail leading to a great treasure. Perhaps my masters wished to claim it for the empire's glory?"

"You can't," said Herdwin. "This area is ours."

"You wouldn't be the first to try to resist the might of Halvaria."

"This is pointless," said Kasri. "I'm going up top to look around."

"Good idea," replied Herdwin. "Let's hope you can figure out the enemy's true strength."

She climbed the stairs, thinking things through as she went. If Halvaria came in the hundreds, it boded ill for the Dwarves of Stonecastle. How could they defeat them yet still get word of the danger to Vard Khazad? She remembered that Herdwin's cousin Gelion marched with a full company of warriors, but would that be enough to stop the invaders? There was much in their favour, including several narrow ledges that would prove difficult for the enemy to assault, yet she couldn't believe only fifty warriors could hold on forever. This army needed to be stopped, and the sooner, the better.

She reached the top floor, then found the ladder leading to the roof. It was dangerous to go outside, for if they spotted her, she might find herself the target of archers. Better, then, to keep as hidden as possible. To that end, she climbed up and lifted the hatch to peek outside. The sun would soon be hidden behind the mountains, making it all the more critical she observe the enemy now while she still could.

Kasri carefully opened the hatch the rest of the way, making no sound. The edge of the tower hid her presence, so she crawled over and peered at the men below. A sizable force had arrived, consisting of riders and many archers. With any hope of getting to the bridge now dashed, a burst of anger seized her. This land belonged to the Dwarves; how dare they attempt to claim it as their own!

She began counting warriors, but additional sounds from the east signified the presence of an even larger force approaching. Kasri crawled to the eastern side of the roof and beheld a sight that would forever live on in her memory.

A column of warriors stretched out along the road as far as the eye could see. Even a conservative estimate would put their numbers at nearly five hundred—this was no ordinary scouting mission! She returned to the ground floor disheartened.

Herdwin looked up as she entered the room. "Any news?"

"Nothing good, I'm afraid. It looks like Darfal told us the truth."

"How badly are we outnumbered?"

"I'd say at least two hundred to one," she replied.

"Is that all? I expected more."

"Make jokes if you must," said Darfal, "but you will not live much longer unless you surrender."

"He's awfully keen for us to throw down our weapons," said Herdwin. "He doesn't know us Dwarves very well."

"And what is that supposed to mean?"

"It means," replied Kasri, "that we mountain folk don't surrender."

The prisoner shrugged. "It matters little in the long run. Our glorious army will kill you and then continue up this pass."

"They have enough men. Why don't they just keep us locked up here and continue on their way?"

"That's easy," said Herdwin. "This tower commands the pass. Anyone marching past would be subject to a hail of bolts."

"From just the two of us?"

"It only requires one bolt to take down a horse and disable a wagon, thereby clogging the trail. I'm assuming the army has wagons to carry its supplies."

"I wonder," said Kasri. "Do you think their wagons could navigate the bridge? It's extremely narrow in the middle."

"I hadn't considered the possibility. Then again, I didn't expect there'd be a full-blown army waiting for us."

"What shall we do?"

"The first thing is to gag this fellow; I've had about enough of his threats."

"Agreed." Kasri ripped off part of the man's tunic, stuffed it in his mouth, and then tied a strip around his head to keep it in place. "What about this other fellow? The wounded one?"

"He looks to have passed out," replied Herdwin. "But we'll gag him too. The last thing I want is for him to wake up and start blathering on like his friend here."

Kasri inspected the door. "This looks solid enough. I doubt they'll get through it."

"Not unless they have an Earth Mage. Did you see any signs of one when you spotted their army?"

"No, not that I'd have any idea what one would look like, even if I saw one."

"Then how do you know you didn't?"

"Everyone I could see looked like a warrior. Of course, that's no guarantee, but I'll go with my gut instinct."

"Suits me," said Herdwin.

"There were a lot of bolts upstairs, along with a few arbalests. We could always try to pick them off as they pass."

"Probably our best course of action, at least for the moment. How are we for food?"

"You tell me," said Kasri. "How much food do they keep in these towers?"

"Enough to last the garrison at least a month."

"Stonecakes?"

"Aye, which means they won't spoil. I'm more concerned about water, though. There's a barrel up on the top floor, fed by a funnel on the roof. What I don't know is how much rain they've had these last few days, or snow, for that matter."

"We've still got our waterskins. I reckon I've half a day left. You?"

"About the same," said Herdwin.

"You check out the water situation while I take a peek out the second-floor window."

"Very well." Herdwin rushed upstairs. The top floor contained the armoury, with bundles of bolts and half a dozen arbalests just as Kasri had stated. There was also spare armour consisting of a couple of Dwarven chain shirts, helmets, and four wooden shields.

Of more interest to the smith, however, was the water barrel, but he needn't have worried, for it was over three-quarters full, enough to last weeks, even if they chose not to ration themselves. It appeared they would be able to settle in for a long siege.

He gathered some stonecakes and exited the armoury. He'd only descended seven or eight steps when he met Kasri on the way up.

"Problem?" he asked.

"It appears someone is at the door."

"What does he want?"

"To speak to us. I thought it best you do the talking. You're more familiar with the vard's wishes."

"The second floor has two windows facing the front," said Herdwin. "I'll show myself at one, but I want you at the other, along with a couple of loaded arbalests."

"A couple?"

"Yes. That way, you can get two bolts off quickly without worrying about reloading."

Herdwin peered out the window. "Hello, down there!"

Below stood a man dressed in red, his long, grey beard hanging to the middle of his chest, topped off with a tall, red hat, reminding the Dwarf of a Mercerian Holy Father.

His gaze rose to settle on Herdwin. "Good day, Sir Dwarf."

"Who are you that comes begging at my door?"

"One of the emperor's truthseekers, Valdarian by name."

"And what is it you seek, Valdarian?"

"Only to speak on behalf of my emperor. Come. Open the door, and we shall converse."

"I'm afraid I've no time for pleasantries. Speak plainly, and let us be done with this matter as efficiently as possible."

"Very well. My master requests you surrender this tower and all who take shelter within."

"And if I don't?"

"Then the Imperial Army will reduce it to rubble."

"That's a fine boast," said Herdwin, "but this tower is Dwarven-made. I doubt your weapons could do much against it."

Valdarian's gaze roamed across the structure. "I see nothing that indicates it is of exceptional quality. Come now. Let us not waste further bloodshed."

"Why? Because you can't afford to lose the men?"

"I'll have you know these men are more than capable of

reducing your place of refuge. Now, I demand you open this door."

"You demand? What makes you think I would consider such a thing?" Herdwin's gaze flicked to those behind the truthseeker. "Your men are not equipped for a siege. Besides, this place is defended by Dwarves. Do you know so little of our people?"

"We slew the garrison here easily enough. Surrender yourselves before you force us to kill you as well."

"And if we surrendered, what would happen to us?"

"We would take you back to our emperor so he might learn more about your people."

"Why? So he can conquer them?"

"We do not seek to conquer," said Valdarian. "Rather, we liberate."

"As in, you liberate our treasury? I don't think so."

"Surely you must realize your position is hopeless. Surrender now, and we will spare your lives."

"And how do I know I can trust you?"

"I give you my word," replied the Human.

"Your word? For all I know, you might be the type of Human that lies through his teeth. How are we to trust you?"

"Could I offer you a guarantee?"

"I'm listening."

"A portion of gold? You can consider it a reward for speeding along the emperor's plans."

"How much gold?" said Herdwin.

"Half your weight in coins."

"You don't know what I weigh." The Dwarf noticed a

look of annoyance cross the Halvarian's face. Behind him, the mountain's shadow grew longer, and soon, night would be upon them. "Let me talk to my comrades," continued Herdwin. "Perhaps I shall be able to convince them that your offer is made in good faith."

"How long will that take?"

"I don't imagine it'll be too difficult to come up with a solution. Shall we return at dusk to discuss the matter in more detail?"

"Very well," said Valdarian. "As the sun begins to set."

Herdwin closed the shutters.

"You expect to discuss the matter?" said Kasri.

"No, of course not. I'm buying us some time."

"You have an idea?"

"The beginnings of one."

"What are you thinking?"

"First, tell me," said Herdwin. "When you were on the rooftop, were they surrounding the place?"

"No. They camped mainly in front and to the sides. The rear of the tower is close to a sheer drop."

"Here's what I'm thinking. We start by wasting as much time as possible."

"Until the thick of night?"

"Yes, precisely. The plan would be to climb down the back of the tower."

"We have no rope," warned Kasri.

"Not at the moment, but on that rooftop is the pole they use to hoist the signal lantern, which has a rope attached. I'm hoping it's long enough for us to drop to the ground."

"And if they hear us?"

"That is a problem. How are you at climbing? You're not afraid of heights, are you?"

"No. I'm a dragon rider, remember?"

"Oh yes. Sorry."

"Once we're on the ground, how do we escape?"

"That's another issue. We'll need to sneak past the enemy camp. I'm gambling they won't sleep too close to the edge for fear of falling into the ravine."

"So, we climb down quietly, then sneak along the side of the Halvarian encampment. How do we get across Kharzun's Folly?"

"The bridge? I suppose we'll need to fight our way to the other side. Sorry, it's the best I could come up with."

"We're well-armoured," said Kasri, "and there's the advantage of darkness. We'll just have to make do."

"We could stay here if you'd prefer."

"And simply delay the inevitable? I think not."

"Good," said Herdwin. "I was hoping you'd say that. Now, just in case we don't make it, there's something I want to talk to you about."

"No," said Kasri. "Don't say it. Tell me when this is all over."

"And if I die?"

"You're too stubborn to die, especially when so much is left unsaid. That will be what keeps you alive."

"And yourself?"

"I've been a warrior my entire life. I may not have my plate armour, but my spirit is intact, and my hammer ready to do justice to its name. Speaking of which, you must remember one thing."

"Which is?" said Herdwin.

"If I call on Stormhammer, close your eyes, if only for a moment."

"Why?"

"It will soon be nighttime, and when I throw lightning, it'll light up the sky, ruining everyone's ability to see in the dark."

Herdwin laughed. "Good. Then they'll all be stumbling around in confusion. Perhaps, if we're lucky, they'll even fall into the ravine?"

"We must still get to the bridge."

"Agreed, but once we're on it, they can only come at us in small numbers."

"You're assuming they haven't already crossed."

"I am," said Herdwin. "But if I'm wrong, there's not much we can do about it. Besides, we'll be two Dwarves fighting side by side. Who can stand against us?"

"True, and there is no one else I would prefer to be shoulder to shoulder with in these final moments. Let us give the bards something to sing about."

"Speaking of bards, I wonder what Delsaran is up to?"

"He should have met up with Gelion by now," said Kasri. "With any luck, they'll be guarding the other end of the bridge."

"Yes, which means if we make it there, we'll be safe, or at least as safe as we can be, facing an army of hundreds."

"Then let us prepare as best we can. Here." He handed her some stonecakes. "Let's eat while we can. It's likely to be a long night."

· · ·

Dusk came far too quickly for Herdwin's liking. He returned to the window to see a Halvarian warrior waiting below, torch held high.

"Go and fetch your truthseeker," said the Dwarf. "I would speak with him."

"Aye, Master Dwarf." He ran off, the flickering of his torch mingling with those of his fellow countrymen.

It took some time for Valdarian to return. The truthseeker looked up, his escort's lantern illuminating his face.

"I am here, Master Dwarf. Have you taken the matter to your comrades?"

"I have indeed, Lord Valdarian. We discussed it at great length before settling on our decision."

"Which is?"

"Generous as your offer was, I'm afraid we shall have to decline at this point."

"You refuse to surrender?"

"We do, at least for now. There was a prevailing thought that a good night's sleep might lead us to reverse our decision on the morrow. I'm inclined to agree, as my mother always warned me about making hasty decisions."

"You called me here to tell me that?"

"I'm sorry it was not the answer you desire, but my people can be a stubborn lot, particularly when ensconced within a tower like this."

"Yet you feel the light of day might change your mind?"

"I have hope that opinions will change, yes."

"Very well, then I shall call upon you to present yourself once more at dawn. Fail me again, however, and you will regret it."

TWELVE

Escape

AUTUMN 966 MC

In gloomy night they slipped away,
Their fellows for to warn.
But danger lurked within the dark,
By soldiers, weapons borne.

And so, the empire made to shout,
That heroes had escaped.
But smith and warrior fought for life,
In Dwarven armour draped.

Herdwin crouched in the dark. "Ready?"

"As ready as I'll ever be. You?"

"I'd feel a whole lot better if the odds weren't so set against us."

From atop the tower, little could hurt them, yet the

knowledge that potentially hundreds of warriors were waiting to kill them kept their nerves on edge.

Kasri tied off the end of the rope to the bottom of the pole, then peered over the edge. Below was pitch black while the wind wound through the ravine, moaning like some ancient spirit.

"Are you sure we can't go down there?" she asked.

"And how would we get up the other side? We have no climbing gear, and this rope certainly isn't long enough. For Gundar's sake, it'll barely reach the ground from here."

"Very well. Shall we begin?"

He nodded, and then she slowly lowered the rope over the side, trying to avoid making any noise. Soon, none remained in her hands, but neither could tell if it reached the ground on this moonless night.

"I'll go first," said Herdwin, lowering himself over the side.

Kasri waited, watching him disappear into the inky blackness. When the rope went slack, she knew he'd reached the base. She followed his lead, scaling down the wall, her legs wrapped around the rope. The rope ended unexpectedly, leaving her dangling.

"Let go," whispered Herdwin. "You're waist high."

She released the rope, her feet quickly landing on stone. Herdwin gripped her bicep, steadying her.

"Which way?" she asked.

He switched to holding her hand and led her to the corner of the tower. From there, he peered around, surveying the enemy camp. Small fires lit up the entire area, with many of the warriors huddled around them, drawing in what heat they offered, while others laid upon blankets, trying to get some sleep.

Herdwin placed his mouth close to Kasri's ear. "We'll need to skirt the edge of their camp. If we keep low and avoid making any noise, there's a good chance they won't notice us."

"And if they do?"

"Then we fight. Do you remember which direction the bridge is in?"

"Of course. Do you think I can lose my sense of direction that easily?" She went quiet for a moment. "Sorry. My nerves got the better of me."

"It's fine," said Herdwin. "I, too, am on edge. What do you think? Shall we pull forth our shields now, or leave them on our backs?"

"Now. If we find ourselves in a fight, there'll be scant time to act." She readied her shield, its weight reassuring on her arm. "There. That's much better." She glanced at her companion but could see little in such gloom. Her hand shot out, finding his waiting. "You lead."

They moved back from the rear of the tower until a fresh breeze blew up from below. "We'll follow the ravine's edge," said Herdwin as he inched forward.

Kasri knew he was feeling his way along by sliding his feet, a common technique amongst Dwarven miners. It had the advantage of ensuring the footing was secure, but it was a slow process. Part of her balked at the delay, wishing to charge headlong into the enemy camp, but she knew such an act would be the end of them both. Death held no fear for her, it never had, but the thought of losing her life without warning the Dwarves of Stonecastle was just too much to bear. A deep rage bubbled up inside her, not at Herdwin but at these foreigners who threatened this land.

Herdwin halted. All she could do was stand in silence, her ears straining to decipher why. Footsteps echoed nearby. She held her breath, tightening her grip on his hand until Herdwin resumed his slow progress along the ravine's edge.

Her eyes, now accustomed to the darkness, could make out general shapes, but the wind, more than anything, told her they were close to the edge, for it whirled up in eddies and currents, sending stray strands of her hair whipping around.

Their journey continued for what felt like forever until light finally appeared ahead of them. They halted, staring down at Kharzun's Folly, a myriad of torches lit on both sides of the ravine. Her heart almost gave out, for now there was no hope of crossing that bridge without Halvarians swarming them.

Herdwin, as if sensing her fear, moved closer. "Those are Gelion's warriors on the far side," he whispered. "Note how they use lanterns instead of torches?"

Relief flooded through her. Escape was at hand: they needed to cross that bridge, but to do that, they must pass through the enemy. "What now?"

"We wait," he replied. "If we catch them as the sun rises, they'll be half-asleep."

"Surely now would be the better option?"

"While there are torches on the bridge, it still makes for treacherous footing. Better to cross it with enough light to see than slide off into oblivion." He sat down. "Come. Let us wait for the dawn together. It may well be our last."

"Don't say that!" she replied. "We'll both survive this, and then one day, we'll tell our children of our great heroics."

"This solves nothing with the guilds."

"I don't care. I shall forge with you, Herdwin, assuming you're still willing. If that means I give up my position as successor, then so be it."

"You would give all that up for me?"

"In an instant. Your heart is pure; your courage unquestionable—you are, quite simply, the noblest Dwarf I've ever met."

"But you are meant to be vard!"

"I don't care. I prefer to be the forge mate of a simple smith than rule without you."

Herdwin chuckled. "I doubt anyone would ever accuse you of being simple."

"So, do you accept my offer to forge?"

"I do, provided we both survive this ordeal."

"Good. Then we both have something to look forward to."

"And you're sure you won't change your mind once this is all over?"

"Never. My heart is set on you, Herdwin Steelarm. I will accept no other."

"Nor I."

They huddled together, waiting for dawn. Here in the mountains, it would begin as a distant light, creeping out from behind the peaks to throw its rays across the land, leaving long shadows that would serve them well.

Kasri was the first to notice the lightening sky. She nudged Herdwin and pointed, noticing how she could now see the outline of her arm. It wouldn't be long before the rising sun revealed their position.

"It's time," she said.

They rose, weapons and shields at the ready. There would be no more shuffling along in the dark. They would walk with purpose, breaking into a run only when someone discovered their presence.

Side by side, they advanced, Kasri keeping her eyes on the bridge while Herdwin watched left, as only the ravine lay to their right.

Fifty paces, and all remained quiet. Now sixty, but then a shout alerted them of their discovery.

"Run," shouted Herdwin. Dwarves, being relatively short of stature, did not have long legs, so they settled into a steady jog, a speed they could keep up for some time.

An arrow whizzed past as the cry of alarm raced through the enemy encampment. Men hurried to retrieve weapons while the Dwarves kept moving.

A trio of Halvarians blocked their path. Herdwin rushed forward with his shield, smashing into two of them and sending them to the ground. Kasri struck with her hammer, hitting the third's leg, causing her foe to collapse. She ignored his cries of pain, continuing towards the bridge.

Their target drew ever closer, but so, too, did the defenders. Someone, a leader, by the look of his elaborate armour, lined up a group of men in a defensive position, their spears bristling.

Kasri let loose with a bolt of lightning, striking the fellow in the centre of his chest, causing him to stagger back. Perhaps more importantly, though, those on either side retreated in terror. She charged into the opening, her hammer swinging wildly.

Herdwin's axe took a man in the kidneys, puncturing his armour and sending blood spurting. He drew back his weapon, ready for another strike, just as a spear scraped along his chain shirt, but the Dwarven links held. The smith's shield came down, driving the spear's tip into the ground, and then his axe severed the hand holding the enemy weapon in place.

Their initial charge broke through, but as the shattered line fell behind the Dwarves, more Humans appeared before them. Soon, Herdwin and Kasri were once more in melee, surrounded by the enemy.

Stormhammer struck out again and again, occasionally loosing bolts of lightning, but the Halvarians were everywhere. Beside her, Herdwin fought on, his axe covering the ground in blood. Their progress slowed, even as the enemy backed up.

The sun poked its head between two peaks, flooding the area in daylight. The Halvarians formed yet another new line in front of them, into which the retreating men took refuge. Kasri glanced over her shoulder to see a similar scene behind them. They were now truly trapped between a hammer and an anvil.

"For Gundar's sake," shouted Herdwin. "We're surrounded!"

"Surrender!" called out a familiar voice. The men parted, revealing the truthseeker, Valdarian. "You've had your fun, but I'm afraid it's time to quench the flame of resistance. Surrender yourselves, and your deaths will be merciful."

"And if we don't?" said Herdwin.

"You shall be put to a slow and painful end."

"We still have our weapons," shouted a defiant Kasri, "and Dwarves don't surrender!"

"A pity," replied the Human. "It would've been interesting to see how long you could withstand our interrogation methods."

"Enough of this," said Kasri. "Stand aside, and we will be on our way."

"Have you learned nothing of our ways? Cease this endless prattling and surrender yourselves to the inevitability of your defeat."

She took a quick look at Herdwin. "What do you think?"

He gripped his axe tightly. "Whenever you're ready."

Kasri held Stormhammer on high, calling on the Gods in the ancient language of their people. Lightning cracked through the sky to envelop the weapon's head, lighting it up like the brightest of lanterns. She flung out her arm, sending the power rushing towards the truthseeker, striking him square in the face, and his entire body lit up. In a flicker, the lightning left, leaving a burned head atop a body that soon went limp.

The spectacle stunned the Halvarians while the Dwarves rushed forward, weapons ready to strike. Three steps, then four, and suddenly one of the enemy warriors crumpled to the ground, a bolt lodged firmly in his back. Others turned, eager to discover the source of this fresh attack.

Herdwin hit them hard, using his shield to significant effect. With enemies ahead of and behind them, the enemy line rapidly disintegrated. On the far side of the bridge, a Dwarven cheer arose as Gelion's arbalesters poured bolt after bolt into the hostile forces.

Kasri grabbed Herdwin's arm, pulling him across the centre span, their opposition having melted away. A group of mailed Dwarves met them, parting their line to allow them entry, and once through, Herdwin collapsed.

"Are you injured?" said Kasri.

"No, just out of breath. I can't believe we made it!" He staggered to his feet. Dwarves swarmed them both, patting them on the back and offering hands in greeting.

"Well, Cousin," said Gelion. "It appears you've been busy."

"You made it!" said Herdwin.

"Aye, and not a moment too soon, it would appear. Thankfully, the Elf filled us in on what's been happening."

"The Elf?"

"Yes, Delsaran? You told him to wait for us, did you not?"

"I did, but he never crossed the bridge. How, then, did he know what befell us?"

"No doubt those long ears of his, or his eyesight. They say an Elf can see things we Dwarves only imagine. In any case, it's a good thing he was on the alert. He's the one who spied you making a break for it."

"Where do we stand at the moment?"

"The enemy has withdrawn to the far end of the bridge,

while we continue to hold the near side. I suppose you'd call it a standoff of sorts.

"Perhaps," said Herdwin, "but it won't last long. They have the advantage."

"What kind of numbers are we talking about?"

"At least five hundred," said Kasri. "I saw them yesterday from atop the tower. They're spread out along the road to the east."

"They'd still need to cross the bridge," said Gelion. "And my arbalesters will play havoc with their advance."

"True, but eventually, your warriors will run out of bolts, then it will come down to melee."

"Are you suggesting my warriors won't hold?"

"No. I'm sure they'll fight to the death, but even you must realize that the enemy's numbers are destined to overwhelm you."

"Perhaps, but that's a discussion for later. You need to rest while you can, but I need a full report of your discoveries before I send word back to Stonecastle."

"It will take three days at least to reach the vard," said Herdwin. "And another three, maybe even four, for more warriors to arrive. Can we hold out that long?"

"We shall certainly give it a try," said Gelion.

Herdwin opened his eyes to find Kasri staring down at him. "Something wrong?" he asked.

"I was going to wake you, but you looked so peaceful, I didn't want to disturb you."

He smiled. "I'm never disturbed to see you." He sat up,

noting the position of the sun. "Is it noon already?"

"It is."

"And has the enemy attacked?"

"Not yet, but they're increasing their numbers. That's why Gelion sent me to fetch you. He thinks they may be up to something and wants to hear your thoughts on the matter."

"And yours, too, I'd warrant." He accepted her hand to help him to his feet but kept his grip, causing her to meet his gaze. "Were you serious about what you said earlier? About forging, I mean?"

"I was. Why? Are you having second thoughts?"

He smiled. "No, not at all. It's just that… well, I can't believe my ears."

"Come now. You must have realized months ago how I felt about you."

"Oh, I did, and make no mistake, I feel the same about you, but I never expected you to give up the Throne of Iron-cliff for me."

"Nor would I have done so in those days, but the time we spent together these last few weeks has only strengthened my heart. If I have to choose, then I choose you."

Herdwin was at a loss for words. Instead, he grabbed her, holding her in a tight embrace. They stood thus until a cough interrupted them.

"Am I intruding?" asked Delsaran.

"You are," replied Kasri, "but it matters little. We're on our way to speak to Captain Gelion."

"Really? It looked more like you two were—"

"There's no time for idle speculation," interrupted Herdwin. "We must be on our way. Is there something you wanted?"

"Yes. I have almost completed your saga."

"I beg your pardon?"

"Your saga—the song recounting the exploits of you two. My interruption of your intimate moment has given me the perfect ending for my tale."

Herdwin blushed. "That was none of your business."

"So you were not embracing?"

"No, we were," said Kasri, "but what of it? Is it not the custom of Elves to show their affection for each other by such acts?"

"It is, but I believed it rare amongst the mountain folk. From all I have learned, such displays are reserved for those who are to be joined, or rather forged—to use your expression for it."

"Then your observation is correct."

"Meaning?"

"Herdwin and I are to be forged."

The Elf broke into a wide smile. "My dearest congratulations to you both. When is the happy union to be celebrated?"

"That has yet to be determined, and in any case, it's our custom for only the closest friends and family to be present."

"I see. And may I enquire where said ceremony will be performed? I only ask because you come from two very distant places."

"I hadn't thought of that." She looked at Herdwin. "What think you?"

"It would have to be Ironcliff or Wincaster."

"Not Stonecastle?" asked Delsaran.

"No. Stonecastle hasn't been my home for decades."

"Yet you still have family there, yes?"

"I do," said Herdwin, "but they are more than capable of travelling."

"Even as far as Ironcliff?"

"That wouldn't be necessary," said Kasri. "Our master of rock and stone can transport my father to Wincaster."

The answer took Herdwin by surprise. "Are you sure?"

"If I am no longer to be vard, then why stay in Ironcliff? I shall live out my days in Wincaster. I'm sure the queen would be more than willing to take me into her service."

"Of that, I have no doubt, but the war in Merceria is over."

Kasri looked eastward towards the other end of the bridge. "Perhaps, but storm clouds are brewing. It won't be long before they break, and the land finds itself once more in the throes of war."

THIRTEEN

The Bridge

AUTUMN 966 MC

Upon the bridge, the duo stood,
Protecting all the west.
And on came hordes of empire troops,
Advancing line abreast.

Three times was the enemy repulsed,
Their casualties oh so high.
But nothing could dissuade our pair,
From holding, do or die.

They joined Gelion as he waited at the end of the bridge, staring east. Twelve arbalesters stood watch, with ten more warriors close at hand, in case the enemy should attempt an assault.

"I've got him," Kasri announced. "He was still sleeping."

"That's to be expected," replied the captain. "Although I must admit to some surprise that you didn't catch a snooze yourself."

"I did," she replied, "but I'm used to getting by on brief naps."

"What's going on?" asked Herdwin.

"Not much right now," replied his cousin. "They sent a few scouts to the centre, but our bolts drove them back. They appear content to stay on their side for the moment."

"They're likely waiting for their reinforcements to move up."

"No," said Kasri. "They're waiting for darkness. It's the only way to neutralize our arbalesters."

"So," said Gelion, "you think they'll try a direct assault?"

"With numbers like that, I suspect it's inevitable."

"They'll take heavy losses."

"I doubt they care," offered Herdwin. "They're fanatical, each one glad to give their life in service to their emperor."

"Even so, it would surely play havoc with their morale."

"You underestimate their zeal. We held two of them prisoner in that tower over yonder, and neither one even broke a sweat."

"What's their armour like?"

"Nowhere near as good as Dwarven mail, at least not the provincials we saw. They might, however, have better-equipped warriors following along behind."

"Are there any bowmen?" asked Gelion.

"There are, although nothing like our arbalests."

"I would concur," said Kasri. "From what I saw, their bows are similar to what the Mercerian archers employ. Not the longer weapons the rangers use, mind, but the shorter variety employed by the bulk of their bowmen."

"Thank Gundar, for small favours."

"What's your plan?" asked Herdwin.

"For the moment?" replied Gelion. "Stand and keep them from crossing. I sent word to Stonecastle, but I expect nothing in reply until at least the end of the week. I'm afraid we're all on our own. We could fall back to the next tower, I suppose."

"And surrender the bridge? I don't believe that's wise. For one thing, you'd never be able to fit your entire company into one of those towers, and for another, you'd be giving up the biggest tactical advantage you possess, namely that bridge."

"Agreed, but as Kasri pointed out, our bolts won't last forever, and our warriors, as skilled as they are, can't fight an endless battle."

"What if we destroyed the bridge?" asked Kasri. "Is there any other way across?"

"Not without climbing down the ravine and back up, and it would take some skilled mountaineers to do that. Do they have such men?"

"If they do, I saw no sign of it. What of the bridge itself? Can it even be destroyed?"

"Yes," said Herdwin. "When we first crossed it, I examined that centre span. There's a keystone holding up the middle. Destroy that, and the entire thing will collapse."

"And how does one do that?" asked Gelion.

"With a pick, ideally. Have you any amongst your warriors?"

"We do. Several, in fact. They're great against heavily armoured opponents. What have you got in mind?"

"That centre span is narrow, only wide enough for a single person, but it is very sturdy, requiring a lot of work to break that keystone. With enough warriors, we could swap people out and do the maximum amount of damage in the shortest amount of time."

"But when do we do this?" asked Kasri. "Moving up in broad daylight will make us susceptible to the enemy's bows."

"Yes," added Gelion. "Do so at night, and we could stumble into their assault."

Herdwin considered the options. "There might be an alternative. What if we set out at dusk?"

"Will that be enough time to bring down the bridge before they attack?"

"Possibly. I can't say for certain."

"Hold on a moment," said Kasri. "What risk is there to the person who breaks the keystone? Does the bridge collapse immediately, or will they have a warning that it's about to go?"

"That's an excellent question. The truth is, I don't really know. I'm a smith, not an engineer." He turned to Gelion. "I don't suppose any of your warriors spent time in the engineering guild?"

"I can find out easily enough," replied his cousin.

· · ·

Kasri moved to the cliff's edge, peering down into a ravine full of mist. With the bottom obscured, only the rushing water echoing off the stone walls indicated a river ran far below.

"Deep, isn't it?" said Herdwin. "I shouldn't like to trip; I doubt anyone would survive a fall like that. Have you such things back in Ironcliff?"

"No, at least not in the city. As I've said before, the great doors of the city open onto a plain."

"I should very much like to see it someday."

"And you will," said Kasri. "I'll take you to meet my father."

"So he can size me up?"

"No, so I can show you off. You've got nothing to be ashamed of, Herdwin. Nothing at all."

"Yet I shall ever bear a grudge against the smiths guild, for they forced you to choose between the Crown of Iron-cliff and me."

"Nonsense. You are my future. The Throne is nothing but an empty promise."

"You say that now, but what about your father?"

"He'll be upset, naturally, but he knows once I make up my mind, there's nothing he can do to change it." She chuckled. "I imagine it'll give him a headache trying to decide on a new successor, if only because the guilds will suggest their own people for the role."

"It's a shame, really. You would have made a wonderful vard."

"To be honest, I enjoy being a warrior more. And look at

all I've accomplished: I commanded the Hearth Guard, led the army of Ironcliff, even rode a dragon, for Gundar's sake. Yet all of those things pale compared to the thought of spending the rest of my life with you."

"And you won't regret giving up all those other things?"

"No, in fact, quite the reverse. When you agreed to forge with me, I felt my spirit lifted, as if Haldur's forge itself burned within my heart."

"I felt the same," said Herdwin. "You know, it's strange, but I thought I'd spend my entire life alone. I suppose that's why I moved to Wincaster—it's not as if I'd be missing anything. Then you came along and changed everything. Now, the future looks bright again, despite this whole debacle with the guild."

"I've seen your workshop, but what's your home like?"

"Not as roomy as you might imagine, but there's plenty of space for expansion. It sits beneath my forge, but we could also live aboveground in the Human style, if you prefer?"

"Now that the Mercerians have learned how to make plate armour, you may need to enlarge your workshop, perhaps even construct a new one. I doubt many smiths in Merceria can work metal in such a manner."

He smiled. "Only one I know of, aside from myself, of course."

"I expect you'll be busy in the coming months. The Queen of Merceria must be eager to equip her finest warriors with the best armour."

"Doubtless, but I shall make time to visit Ironcliff. After

all, I can't carry off their most precious jewel without at least meeting them."

"What jewel is that?"

"You, of course."

"It seems not only are you a master smith but a bard as well. Is this Delsaran's influence?"

"Perhaps."

Gelion returned, slightly out of breath. "Well, it's official —the Gods have turned their backs on us."

"Meaning?" said Kasri.

"None of my men were ever engineers or architects, for that matter. I'm afraid we're on our own."

"You're in command, Captain. What do you want to do?"

"We'll go with Herdwin's suggestion, even though it means picking away at the span while in sight of the enemy. It's risky, but it gives us the best chance of halting these invaders once and for all."

"Couldn't they build another bridge?"

"Possibly, but with what? They'd need to bring lumber from miles away, and we'll keep a permanent garrison here after this. Who knows, we might even build a fortified wall to block our side of the ravine. All I know is, once that bridge is down, those men over there have no way of attacking, at least not in the short term."

"And in the long term?"

Gelion shrugged. "Winter will soon be upon us, and those troops don't look prepared for cold weather. I expect they'll choose to retreat."

"Assuming we can break the bridge," said Herdwin.

"Right now, it's all conjecture on my part. What if I'm wrong?"

"We must work on the assumption you're not. Logic dictates that breaking that span, even just a small part of it, will make their attack that much more difficult."

"Then we wait for dusk."

Kasri listened as a haunting tune carried across the camp, the unmistakable voice of Delsaran, rising above the hubbub of the Dwarven warriors. It felt surreal, for such things were done at court, not an army camp, yet it somehow fit the occasion. Tension was building, for everyone knew what was coming. The work of destroying the bridge would commence as soon as the sun began its descent behind the mountains.

Even though the chance of survival was slim, every single member of Gelion's company volunteered. However, only three were chosen in the end, and they, along with Herdwin, would pick away at the centre span while the others behind them attempted to hold the enemy back with carefully placed arbalest bolts. It was not an ideal plan, for darkness would soon make such volleys impractical, but Kasri waited with another group of warriors ready to charge forward.

The biggest flaw in the plan was the bridge itself, for to protect those picking away at the keystone, Kasri's small contingent had to cross the span, meeting the enemy on their side. Once the bridge began to give way, they had to retreat or be trapped on the other side.

The centre arch's narrowness added to the danger, for they could only cross it one at a time. Herdwin had to watch the keystone carefully for this to succeed. They intended to call the retreat as soon as cracks appeared, but she had doubts such things would be easy to spot once the dark of night enveloped them.

The song ended, leaving Kasri with an incredible feeling of loneliness. Dwarves surrounded her, yet without Herdwin's presence, she felt as if a part of her were missing.

When she spotted him walking towards her, her heart swelled. "It's about time you showed up."

"Sorry," replied the smith. "I was going over details with the other pick wielders. We decided to use a lantern to illuminate the span while we work."

"That will mark you as a target!"

"It will, but how else are we to tell when the cracks appear? The last thing we want to do is bring the bridge down while we're standing on it."

"The enemy arrows will target the lantern holder."

He grinned. "Ah, but we thought of that. We'll suspend the light from a long pole. That way, the holder can be away from where the digger works."

"And how long will that take?"

"It's difficult to say. The keystone lies at the centre of the arch, but we must dig through the top of the span to get to it. To make matters worse, they built the entire bridge to be able to withstand a lot of punishment."

"That's typical of Dwarven construction, isn't it?"

"It is," agreed Herdwin. "And ordinarily, that would be a good thing, but it works against us in this instance. The truth is this entire operation could take all night. Then again, it could just as easily be over with two or three swings of a pick."

"Well then, we shall keep you safe while you work. For the moment, however, you should rest. You're going to need all the strength you can muster."

"I'm too anxious to sleep, but we could always talk to while away the time."

"I would like that."

"What shall we do once this is all over?"

"I thought we already decided to settle down in Wincaster?"

"No, I'm talking about the immediate future."

"I assumed we'd make our way back to Stonecastle," she said. "The vard will no doubt want a full recounting of everything."

"After that, I thought we might linger for a few days so you can meet all my cousins."

"I would like that. Are they all to be invited to our forging?"

"Of course, though I doubt many would make the journey to Wincaster. As to witnesses, I thought I might ask Gerald to stand in. I know it's not common for an outsider to perform such a task, but he's one of my closest friends."

"That's an excellent idea."

"And what of yourself?"

"I shall ask Dame Beverly to stand by my side. I think it only fitting since we are to make our lives in Merceria, don't you?"

"I do, but I wonder if we should invite the queen?"

"Nonsense. A forging is a personal matter, not the big ceremonies Humans are so fond of. We should not throw all of our traditions into the fire, only the ones that annoy us."

"You mean like supporting guilds?"

"Exactly."

Herdwin laughed. "I suppose we should start making a list."

"A list?"

"Yes, which customs to keep and which to get rid of."

Delsaran's voice called out. "What are you two up to?"

"Making plans," said Kasri.

"About the attack?"

"No, our forging."

"Oh yes. I am most curious to learn more. Tell me, what are your customs in this regard? Do you stand before a Holy Father, like they do in Merceria, and recite an oath?"

"No, religion is a personal choice amongst us. Thus, we consider it more of a… what would you call it?"

"A civil union," added Herdwin. "A promise between two people."

"And do Dwarves wear rings to signify their joining?" asked Delsaran.

"No. During the ceremony, we both break open nuggets of metal that will later be formed into a single item of some sort."

"To what end?"

"It signifies the union and is displayed in a prominent place within the home."

"What kind of item?"

"It could be anything," said Kasri. "My parents forged

theirs into a cup. They would drink from it on special occasions."

"Yes," said Herdwin, "and mine made a knife out of theirs to use when cutting meat."

"So, these things always have a practical purpose?" asked the Elf.

"Most of the time, but some individuals prefer something more decorative."

"Such as?"

"A metal plate displayed on the wall, or even something more unique. My cousin created a sculpture of Gundar's head."

"That must have taken an inordinate amount of work?"

"Aye, it did," said Herdwin, "and more's the pity; the forging only lasted a few years."

"She died?"

"No, but she grew tired of his incessant demands and annulled their relationship. We call it unforging, though sometimes the term quenched is used."

"Is that common?"

"Common? No, but certainly not unheard of."

"And there is no one to officiate this quenching?"

"No. Only witnesses to record it."

"And is that true of a forging as well?"

"A forging is a little different," said Kasri. "It usually calls together friends and families to celebrate the occasion. Although it requires only two witnesses to make it official, there are often many more."

"You are a strange people," said the Elf. "Sorry. That is

not to imply you are in any way inferior, merely... different."

"What is the Elven custom?"

"That is not typically discussed with outsiders, although I can tell you it is not too dissimilar to Human customs, from what I know. We exchange vows before witnesses, but unlike the custom of your people, we consider it a religious ceremony. Of course, if you tell anyone I revealed that, I shall deny it, but it is the truth. I swear."

"Why are Elves so secretive?" asked Herdwin.

The bard looked back in surprise. "Why would we be anything but? We hide our lands to avoid invasion, and our people remain hidden amongst the trees for their own safety. Without children, our numbers will only dwindle, so we make every effort to keep ourselves as far away from death as possible."

"And yet you helped the Mercerians."

"Only after remaining neutral for quite some time. In the end, Lord Arandil thought it best to act. You have his daughter, Telethial, to thank for that. Had she not died fighting for the Mercerians, I doubt any other Elven warriors would ever have left the safety of the Darkwood."

Kasri nodded towards the far side of the ravine. "And if those Halvarians decide to attack Stonecastle, would he come to their aid?"

"I think he would," said Delsaran. "Though I warn you, I am in no way privy to his personal opinions on the matter."

"Then what makes you believe he would?"

"For centuries, the Darkwood retained strong trade links with the mountain folk, and now that both served together in war, I believe it unlikely they would break those ties. On another matter, the destruction of Stonecastle would leave the Darkwood dangerously exposed. From our point of view, the only downside is that the terrain hereabouts is not exactly the type Elves are used to fighting in."

"Let's hope we can end it here, and then we'll all be spared the horrors of war."

FOURTEEN

Kharzun's Folly

AUTUMN 966 MC

The bridge of stone, of Dwarf king past,
Withheld throughout the day.
Yet all upon it knew that soon,
Their foe would have its way.

And so, upon the central arch,
Did Herdwin make his stand.
And there was Kharzun's Folly,
Destroyed by hero's hand.

erdwin hefted the pick, the weight different from what he was used to—far heavier than his customary axe. Three other Dwarves stood beside him, all armed similarly. He watched Gelion lining up the warriors who would advance, sending a hail of bolts flying towards the enemy.

Off to one side waited Kasri with six warriors. It would be their job to prevent the Halvarians' advance, but first, they needed to get across the centre span.

Gelion gave the command, and everyone started their assigned tasks. Bolts sailed forth, more as a warning than doing any actual damage to the enemy. Kasri's troops moved up to cross the centre span, their mere presence forcing the Halvarian pickets back. Once on the other side, however, they became targets of Halvarian arrows. Shields created a wall that soaked up the enemy's volleys.

With everyone now in place, Herdwin moved up with his fellow pick wielders, soon reaching the centre span. Herdwin took the first swing, testing the nature of the beast. Though no stone flew, he spotted a hairline crack in one of the slabs making up the bridge's surface. He quickly got to work, hefting the pick with all the strength he could muster.

There was no time to think about the enemy, only chipping away at the bridge. After many swings, a small stone fragment was all he had to show for his work. Clearly, this would take a while. He bent his back to the task, soon losing all sense of time.

Kasri watched the enemy closely. After their initial volleys, the Halvarians settled for keeping an eye on the Dwarves from a distance. She knew it wouldn't last. Once they realized what Herdwin was up to, they would swarm the bridge, desperate to put an end to the work.

Her warriors held steel-rimmed wooden shields with many of the enemy's arrows sticking in them, making them look like porcupines. She gave the order, and they plucked the arrows loose one by one, always on the lookout for any sign of advance.

The enemy's area was well-lit, and thanks to their over-abundance of torches, she could see men wandering around their camp. No one appeared to be in a hurry, yet the glint of armour told her something was happening.

"They're donning their mail," she said, more to herself than to any of her command. "I expect the enemy to form up before trying anything, but keep your eyes on them. They might surprise us."

"Let them come," said Belnik as he stood, hefting his mace. "I need to smash in some heads."

"Or any other part of their anatomy," joked Thalbek, his voice echoing inside his pot helm.

It was good to see them in such high spirits, but Kasri wondered how they would fare after their first brush with the enemy. She glanced over her shoulder where Herdwin had stepped back for a rest, leaving one of his companions to take his turn.

"Something's happening," said Belnik.

His words brought Kasri's attention back to the enemy, now formed into a two-rank line, all armed with spears, presenting a wall of steel tips.

The Dwarves held up their shields, their muscles tensing in anticipation. She knew the enemy posed little danger to them, for Dwarven mail was difficult to penetrate, and the mountain folk's superior strength made them capable of inflicting far more damage against their opponents.

Kasri was well aware of the reputation of her people, yet her service with the Mercerians had taught her Humans could often surprise their opponents with their tenacity.

"Watch yourselves," she warned.

The enemy leader barked out a command, and their line advanced in perfect step. They progressed slowly while maintaining their formation, keeping the tips of their spears aligned with the Dwarves' chests. Her troops stood ready, disciplined enough not to break their own formation.

"Shield wall," she ordered, and the Dwarves all shifted slightly, letting their shields interlock.

"Do you know the Iron Coil?"

"Of course," said Belnik. "Gelion has us practice it all the time."

"Good. Then that's what we'll do. Prepare to advance." Everyone gripped their weapons tighter.

Warriors armed with spears usually pulled back on the weapon right before impact so they could thrust as they stepped, thus giving them the extra strength to puncture mail. The Dwarven manoeuvre, called the Iron Coil, counteracted this tactic but had to be timed to perfection. It all came down to discipline, which was something her new command had no shortage of.

The enemy drew closer and closer, then came the instant that makes or breaks an attack. The Halvarian warriors pulled back their spears in preparation for that final thrust, and that's when the Dwarves struck.

Into the Halvarian ranks they stepped, spear tips knocked aside. Shields bashed chests, all thoughts of inter-locking them gone, and then axes and maces struck out. The brutal counterattack took the enemy completely by surprise, and years of training made it much more effective.

Four Humans went down as the lines clashed before the Halvarians found their courage. Spear tips jabbed out, one of them taking Belnik in the bicep. His mace fell to the ground, his weapon arm useless, but Kasri spotted his anger. She grabbed his cloak and heaved him back, using her shield to take the force of the next thrust. She stepped into the new gap, striking out with Stormhammer to break a spear in two and drive her weapon into a forearm.

The ferocity of the attack pushed the enemy back a couple of paces, but then the empire's superior numbers carried them onward. A spear grazed Kasri's helmet, and she struck upward with her hammer, knocking it aside as the Human withdrew his weapon, exposing the poor fool. A step forward with an overhead swing brought her weapon down onto her foe's shoulder, and even through Stormham-mer's grip, she could feel bone breaking. The spear wielder released an agonizing scream and then fell, taking out the man to his left.

With a quick word of command, Kasri sent lightning arcing out before her. No one dropped from the attack, but she smelled burnt flesh, and then some threw down their spears and ran away, screaming in fear.

Thalbek's axe dug into a man's elbow, and his arm went limp. He followed up with another strike, sinking the edge of his weapon into the fellow's side. His foe fell, but such was the force of his attack that the axe blade lodged in his victim's ribs, threatening to disarm the Dwarf.

Out of nowhere came Belnik, and having somehow recovered his mace, he knocked the Halvarian to one side, covering his comrade, even as Thalbek struggled to pull his weapon free.

Kasri took down another attacker, and then the rest of the Halvarians broke and ran, seeking the safety of their side of the ravine.

"Hold!" called out Kasri. Her small command reformed their line.

"Is anybody hurt?" She looked at each in turn. "Belnik?"

"Just a scratch," he replied. "He took me by surprise."

"We'll move back three paces. Keep your formation."

They stepped back while still facing the enemy. Half the attackers lay dead, their blood running to either side of the bridge, emptying into the ravine below.

"Is that all they've got?" said Thalbek.

"That was only their first attack," said Belnik. "There's lots more where that lot came from."

"He's right," said Kasri. "So stay alert."

"Here come more archers," said Belnik.

Kasri squinted, but it was hard to make out much detail in this light. The torchlight showed several bowmen moving up, but she couldn't count them.

"Shields up," she shouted. "And kneel."

Each Dwarf knelt, their shields facing out but angled slightly upward, enough to guard their faces against the volley, effectively reducing the target for the enemy.

When they did come, many of the arrows rattled off

steel helms while others stuck into shields. Kasri felt a slight prickling on her shoulder and noted that an arrow had struck her mail but failed to penetrate and now hung like some macabre fashion statement. She pulled it free while keeping her eyes on the enemy as best she could.

The Halvarians changed their tactics, using the archers' volleys to keep the Dwarves behind cover. Kasri peered out to see more men forming up, this time armed with swords and shields—these were no mere provincials.

"We seem to have impressed them," she said. "They decided to send their best."

"Same again?" asked Thalbek.

"No. I doubt it would work a second time, and in any event, they're armed with swords, not spears."

"They'll have difficulty cutting through our mail with swords."

"True, but how about we let them discover that for themselves?"

They tensed once more, ready to continue the fight.

Herdwin looked up from where he stood, holding a pole from which dangled a lantern, the only way to light the work area without getting in the way. To the east, he heard fighting, but the bridge's centre arch hid his view of it.

Ragnus moved up beside him. "Give me the pole," he said. "It's time for you to return to digging."

Herdwin passed it over, then hefted the pick and moved up to stand in the centre of the bridge. His small group had already dug out a sizeable chunk of the surface, and one further strike revealed the keystone. He knelt, then motioned for the light to be lowered, the better to see what lay beneath.

The keystone was slate grey, easily distinguishable from the lighter-coloured path above. He moved, peering over the edge of the bridge, eager to estimate how thick the keystone might be. But the angle, in conjunction with the difficulty in illuminating the underside, made any estimation impossible.

He returned to his place, hefted the pick on high and brought it down. A tiny chip flew forth, and he knelt again, using his fingers to feel for damage.

"Any luck?" called out Ragnus.

"We've dug down to the keystone, but it shows no signs of cracking."

"Well, it wouldn't, would it?"

"What's that supposed to mean?"

"The keystone will be made of the strongest stone as it has to bear the weight of the bridge."

"And you don't think you should have mentioned this earlier?"

Ragnus shrugged. "I thought it was common knowledge."

"Can we destroy it?"

"Of course, but it's not so much a question of can as when?"

"And your estimate would be?"

"Could be a while yet. Then again, you might get lucky and crack through it in one blow."

"You're not being much help," said Herdwin. "I need to

call the others back before we break through this. Am I going to have some clue when it's about to shatter?"

"Maybe yes, maybe no." Ragnus paused a moment. "Look, you served in the mines, didn't you?"

"I did."

"So, think of it not so much as a keystone but as a piece of granite."

"Refresh my memory as to what that means?"

"They say each stone has its own internal structure lines. Sometimes you get lucky, and it cracks wide open, while other times, it takes longer. Just keep whaling at it. It's bound to give way sooner or later."

"You're a great help," said Herdwin. Each time he struck, the impact reverberated up his arms. A small chip leaped up and hit his cheek, drawing blood, but he ignored it, concentrating instead on hefting the pick over and over.

His arms grew tired, but he became lost in the repetitive actions despite the effort required. The entire task became one endless rhythm, never ending yet never quite completing.

A loud crack broke through his reverie. He had his pick raised overhead before the sound finally registered in his brain. He put down his tool, then crouched, waving for the lantern to be lowered.

The tip of the pick had punctured a hole in the keystone, and large flakes of stone had flown off, exposing a series of small cracks beneath.

Herdwin immediately stood, then turned to look at

Ragnus. "It worked," he said. "The keystone has finally cracked."

"Best get the others back before it breaks."

The smith looked eastward to where the sound of fighting had receded, an eerie silence replacing it.

"Kasri," he called out. "Can you hear me?"

"I hear you."

"Call your warriors back. We need you on this side."

"How long have we got?"

"You must come now—I've already cracked the keystone. I don't know how much longer it will hold up."

He heard her giving orders, then her Dwarves appeared out of the darkness, moving in single file.

Herdwin backed up, letting them pass. Kasri brought up the rear, pausing before him. "Be careful," she warned. "They're massing for another attack."

"Get yourself back to safety, so I can finish this once and for all."

She withdrew to where Gelion and the rest of the company waited.

Herdwin looked at Ragnus. "You, too, my friend."

"But you need the lantern."

"Leave it upon the bridge. You don't have to stay here and hold it." His comrade set it down, then his footsteps receded.

Herdwin took a deep breath before raising his pick once more. He was just about to bring it crashing down when he heard the roar of a crowd girding itself for action.

Ignoring their shouts, he struck the stone, seeing a sizeable chunk slough off. Shapes loomed out of the darkness, and a large Human rushed forward, his sword held high.

Herdwin swung at the fellow's legs, feeling the shaft of the pick hit the man's shin. It didn't penetrate the armour but sent the fellow off balance. In the narrow confines of the centre span, the fool had nowhere to go but over the side, screaming as he fell until the roar of water below swallowed his voice.

After swinging the pick, Herdwin lost his balance, stumbling to his knees in an attempt to remain on the bridge. He glimpsed another individual towering over him, and then he pushed the end of his pick out, using the head like a battering ram into the fellow's stomach. He, too, toppled over the side of the bridge, and that's when Herdwin realized why his people never saw fit to put railings here.

He stood and struck the keystone again, a large chunk coming loose. A fresh breeze blew up from the new hole, indicating significant damage to the structure. It would likely take only a hit or two before he destroyed the keystone.

Another figure advanced, wielding a mace that struck quickly, knocking him from his feet. Herdwin almost lost his pick, recovering it just before it dropped into the ravine. He kicked out desperately and had the satisfaction of knocking out his opponent's ankle. Unfortunately, the Human fell atop him, crushing the breath from his lungs.

The Halvarian rained down blows on him, but between gripping the pick and hanging onto the edge of the bridge to avoid slipping, the Dwarf could do little but lie there and take it.

Another Human appeared above the first, raising his spear for the killing blow. In desperation, Herdwin grabbed his initial assailant and pulled him to one side, directly into the attack of his fellow warrior. The fellow let out a wail of agony as the spear dug into his shoulder, and then Herdwin kicked upward with all his might. His attackers were so tightly packed that they both fell back, and then the second fellow's foot went over the edge. His spear now forgotten, he reached out, grabbing his comrade's belt, but the action took them both over the side.

Herdwin rolled onto his stomach, then rose into a crouch, preparing for his final strike.

Kasri, having reached Gelion's position, turned around to witness the Halvarians attack on Herdwin. She tried to rush back to his side, but a firm hand gripped her arm before she took a step.

"No," shouted Gelion. "It's too late!"

The lantern illuminated the area like some macabre scene of a play, and she watched in horror as the pick came down, and then once more, enemy warriors advanced, threatening Herdwin. A spear reached out, driving into the Dwarf's chest. He staggered back under the blow but then raised his pick and slammed it down onto the stone. For a moment, nothing happened, then a loud pop was immediately followed by a crumbling noise, as though an avalanche were coming.

Kasri held her breath as the bridge collapsed beneath the Human's feet. The Halvarian fell from sight, and then

Herdwin appeared briefly, desperately reaching out for purchase before the centre span gave way, and then he, too, disappeared into the night.

The rumble grew louder, and Gelion pulled her back from the edge of the bridge. Moments later, the entire construction collapsed, dropping into the mist of the ravine.

FIFTEEN

Broken Heart

AUTUMN 966 MC

The land was safe, the enemy dead,
The threat, a blunted knife.
Yet in the moment of triumph great,
Did Herdwin give his life.

So weep for Kasri Ironheart,
Whose spirit thence was broken.
For still she wanders mountain peaks,
Her future left unspoken.

D awn revealed the success of the collapse, for nothing remained of Kharzun's Folly but a vast chasm and tons of rock below, hidden by the mist. Gelion moved up beside Kasri, who'd stayed there all night, staring into the void.

"He gave his life to save us all," said the captain, but she wasn't listening.

All her days, she'd sworn never to forge, only to stumble across the one Dwarf in the entire land who could steal her heart. Now he was dead, crushed by tons of rock and stone. It hurt to breathe, and she knew she would never be free from the pain of Herdwin's loss.

"Come," said Gelion. "We must return to Stonecastle. The vard will expect a full accounting of events."

"No," she replied. "I will stay here and let my body wither where my heart died this night."

"He would not wish you to suffer so."

She turned on him in a fury. "Don't tell me what he would or would not do!"

Gelion backed up in the face of her rage. "I mean no offence, but there is nothing you can do to bring him back. You must be practical about this."

She stared at him, venom in her eyes. He turned and strode off as she returned her gaze to the mist below. Somewhere down there lay what should have been her future: a life shared with love and understanding. Instead, it had all come crashing down in one terrible nightmare, a terror that would live with her for the remainder of her days.

"Mistress Kasri?" Delsaran drew closer.

She turned to the Elf with lifeless eyes. "He was the fire in my hearth," she said, her voice cracking. "The promise of a future shared. Why did he have to die?"

He moved closer, placing his hand on her shoulder. "The Gods are fickle," he soothed. "You could have done nothing to stop it."

"I should have died trying to save him."

"Do you believe he would have wanted that? Herdwin Steelarm was a Dwarf full of life, and he wanted that for you too. Mourn his loss, if you must, but know that, in his heart, he did this for you."

"For me? What are you talking about? He did this to save Stonecastle."

"Perhaps, but he would never have travelled here were it not for you."

"Are you trying to soothe me or cover me in blame?"

"Neither," said the Elf. "You do not understand what I mean."

"Then why don't you try explaining it to me?"

"Your fates were entwined the day you met," said the Elf. "Had you not convinced him to go to Stonecastle, these invaders might have made it through these mountains. You and he were a team, each playing your part."

"I would prefer we'd never met."

"Because the pain is so great?"

"No," she spat out, "because he'd still be alive. Better to have him in the land of the living, even if it meant we never knew each other."

"You mountain folk are difficult to comprehend," said Delsaran.

"You loved Telethial," said Kasri. "Surely you understand loss?"

"I do, all too well, yet unlike you and Herdwin, she did not reciprocate my love. I still feel her loss greatly, but never have I seen such devotion as between you and the master smith of Wincaster. It breaks my heart just to think of it."

She nodded, unable to speak.

They stood thus for some time, gazing into the mist until Kasri finally broke the silence. "What will you do now?"

"I shall travel with Gelion to Stonecastle," replied the Elf, "but my days amongst your people are numbered. I need to return to my people, to mourn in my own way. What of you?"

"I shall remain here for the time being."

"To what end?"

"I wish to mourn in solitude. It is not an easy thing to give part of yourself to another. Now that he's gone, a piece of me died with him."

A shout caught the Elf's attention. "That is Gelion. We must leave. Are you sure you will be all right by yourself?"

"The enemy cannot cross, and there are plenty of stonecakes in my pack. I shall sit here awhile, and in my mind, I'll live the life he and I would have shared. As for you, Delsaran, I wish you well, but you must go and leave me to my solitude. Dwarves prefer to grieve in isolation."

"Farewell, Kasri Ironheart. I hope our paths cross again."

The day wore on. Eagles flew overhead, winging their way to warmer climes, yet still, Kasri sat, her eyes glued to the ravine. Hunger gnawed at her, but she had little appetite for food. She wept often, not for his death, but for a future that was never to be, for such is the way of the mountain folk.

A stiff wind settled in by late afternoon, chilling her to the bone. She finally rose, moving closer to the rocks, hoping to find some respite. Gelion's warriors had seen fit to leave behind a firepit, complete with fuel. She tossed one of the strange cubes amongst the coals and struck flint with steel, producing a spark. Moments later, the cube flared to life, warming the coals.

A rock tumbled nearby, and she grabbed her hammer, convinced something stalked her. She stood, back to the flames, letting her eyes drift over the area, but nothing commanded her attention.

Kasri held her breath, lest her own breathing eclipse any sounds. Again, a scrambling off to the right as if some creature were attempting to climb the rocks. She turned to face the ravine. Could the Halvarians have climbed down one side and up the other? She moved closer, cautiously peering into the ravine.

The mist obscured most of it while the late afternoon sun threw shadows, making it even more difficult to make out any details. But then, a slight movement caught her eye —something was down there, ascending the cliff face! Unable to tear her eyes away, she stared, her mind trying to make sense of what it might be.

Another rock came loose, sending a cascade of dirt and stones crashing into the ravine. Then a face broke through the mist, meeting her gaze. It was Herdwin—his cheeks covered in blood, his helmet dented, but there was no mistaking that countenance!

She rushed back to the fire, quickly rummaging through her pack. No rope was at hand, but the straps might prove useful. She got to work, brandishing a knife to cut away the shoulder straps and tie them together. She added her own belt to the line, then returned to the ravine and lowered one end.

The line went taut, and she hauled for all she was worth, straining against the weight until a bloodied arm reached onto the ledge and held fast.

She discarded the line and moved to grasp him, pulling with what little strength remained. His head emerged, then his torso, until all of him was finally safe.

Kasri fell back, her strength depleted. "How in the name of Gundar are you alive?"

Herdwin grimaced at first, obviously in pain, but not enough to stop him from finally smiling. "There's a river down there," he said. "It broke my fall, more or less, but then I nearly drowned."

"And the blood?"

"The bridge fell in after me. I was lucky it didn't crush me."

He coughed, and droplets of red splattered the ground beside him.

"We must get you to help," said Kasri.

"I can't move. The climb has finished me off."

"No. I won't accept that."

"I'm afraid you must. I haven't the strength to continue."

"Then I shall carry you." She got to work removing his armour, then examined his wounds. They were serious: cuts, bruises, broken bones, but Dwarves had survived worse. The freezing weather caused her more concern, but she hoped that it might just be enough to stop him from bleeding to death.

She bandaged him as best she could, then fed him a

stonecake. It was a day's travel to the nearest tower, likely two, carrying an injured Dwarf, yet she would not abandon him. She discarded her own armour, conserving her strength for the task ahead.

"I'll carry you piggyback," she said, "but I'll need to bind your wrists to prevent you from slipping off my back."

He nodded in reply, too exhausted to object. Once she bound his hands, Kasri stood before him, turned around and put his hands over her neck. She then crouched, placed her arms under his knees, and lifted him up.

She'd expected him to be much heavier, but the load was manageable without his armour. She set off, leaving everything else behind, save for Stormhammer, water, and a handful of stonecakes.

She had to put Herdwin down and scout out the path on more than one occasion. She found the ledges particularly challenging, for they were narrow, the footing treacherous, yet somehow, she persevered, encouraged by his constant but raspy breathing.

It must've been close to midnight when she finally halted. The path here was wider, and she found a cluster of rocks to shelter them from the wind. That night, they huddled together for warmth, for she'd brought nothing with which to build a fire.

Morning came far too early, and she opened her eyes to find a thin layer of frost on both of them. Herdwin was groggy yet still answered when she pressed him to talk, certainly a good sign. They each ate a stonecake, then she lifted him once again, determined to bring him to safety.

It was noon when the sentries spotted them. The garrison at the tower sent out a trio of warriors, and they soon bore Herdwin off to a warm fire. Kasri followed, entering the tower and collapsing into a chair, too exhausted to do anything but watch another Dwarf examine Herdwin's wounds.

The garrison commander, an older fellow with a long-forked beard, loomed over her. "You've done a remarkable thing," he said. "You've brought Herdwin back to us, no small feat."

"It was purely an act of selfishness," she replied. "We are to be forged."

He nodded sagely. "Then we will do all we can to ensure he is capable of doing so. Now come, you must rest. You look spent."

"No. If it's all right with you, I shall stay; I do not wish him to be out of my sight until he recovers."

"Very well, I respect your wishes. In the meantime, I sent a messenger off to Stonecastle. I expect the vard will send his master healer once he receives word. In the meantime, I suggest you both rest here. We have food aplenty, and the warmth will do you well. Might I ask where you left your armour?"

"Back at the remains of Kharzun's Folly."

"I'll send a few of my warriors to recover your belongings. In the meantime, let's get some proper food into you, shall we?"

· · ·

The days passed. Kasri grew stronger, but Herdwin showed little sign of improvement. The vard's healer arrived with eight helpers, and between them, they bore Herdwin upon a litter, covered with numerous blankets to ward off the chill.

They trudged through the snow, for winter had come while they waited at the tower. Kasri refused to leave his side, walking the entire way with one hand on his litter.

Once they arrived at the gates of Stonecastle, they took him to the house of his cousin Gelion. There, they fed him a concoction of herbs, and applied poultices to help heal his broken bones.

Days became weeks before Herdwin could finally get up and move around. His walks grew longer each day until he pronounced himself capable of making the trip home to Wincaster.

"You're still too injured," said Kasri.

"And I shall get no better here. In Wincaster, Lady Aubrey can use her magic to heal my injuries."

"And what of us?"

"My guild status is unchanged."

"But you saved Stonecastle from the Halvarians."

"I did, yet the guilds remain stubborn."

"Then let us return to Wincaster and forge there. We shall spend the rest of our lives in each other's company."

"And you're still willing to do that?"

"I am," said Kasri. "And if my father doesn't like it, then it's his loss."

"You should still tell him."

"I will. I promise. Once we're back in Wincaster, I'll

arrange to travel to Ironcliff. At the very least, I can retrieve my best armour and say my goodbyes."

"It pains me that you must give up your family," said Herdwin. "Yet, at the same time, I'm happy we'll share a life together."

"As am I. Now, continue building up your strength, and let me worry about such things, smith of my heart."

The full force of winter embraced them as they left Stonecastle. Gelion, Margel, and six of Herdwin's cousins escorted them to the edge of the Darkwood, where they said their goodbyes. It was a bitter parting, as the entire reason for their trip had failed miserably. Still, Kasri and Herdwin couldn't remain glum for long, walking through the beautiful forest of the Elves.

A few days later, they reached the Last Hope Inn, where, after a warm meal and a good night's sleep, they continued on their way.

Eventually, the walls of Wincaster came into view, and their journey was almost over. They passed through the gate, making their way to the Queen's Arms for some much-needed ale and a bite to eat. They entered to see Dame Beverly sitting with her husband, Aldwin.

"May we join you?" asked Herdwin.

"Of course," replied the knight. "Did you manage to settle things in Stonecastle?"

He smiled. "Yes, and no."

"That's the guild for you," said Aldwin.

"Well, here's a little news you might not be aware of,"

said Herdwin, then turned to Kasri. "Would you do the honours?"

Kasri smiled. "Herdwin and I are to be forged. What you Humans call married."

"Congratulations," said Beverly. "And when is this joyful event to take place?"

"There are arrangements to be made yet," said Herdwin. "And I must fully recover before the ceremony."

"You're injured?"

"Aye, that he is," said Kasri. "He decided to bring an entire bridge down upon himself. It's a long story that we'll share later, but suffice it to say, he's distinguished himself once again."

"I'll get Aubrey to drop by and use her magic on you," said Beverly.

"That would be most appreciated," replied Herdwin. "In the meantime, we'd like to eat. Nothing against stonecakes, but there's nothing like a Mercerian pudding, along with a nice plate of sausages."

The knight turned her attention to Kasri. "And how did you fare?"

"Quite well, all things considered. Still, I must travel back to Ironcliff and settle a few things."

"Such as?"

"Where we're going to live, though that's not the only thing on my mind. My father feels Herdwin hasn't enough guild status for the forge mate of a vard."

"And?"

"And I'm going to tell him I don't care. Herdwin and I

shall forge, and if it means living in Wincaster the rest of our lives, so be it."

"Well, I, for one, will be happy to have you around. Perhaps you'd like to become part of the Queen's Royal Guard?"

"To guard the Palace? I don't think so."

"No, I mean her elite companies. Gerald's been talking about it for some time. His idea is to group all the best, most experienced warriors together as a reserve. Especially, considering our new arrangement with Ironcliff."

"What agreement is that?" asked Kasri.

"Haven't you heard? The queen formally signed a defensive agreement with your father. Merceria and Ironcliff are now officially allies."

"That's good to hear," said Herdwin. "I suppose that means there'll be more mages going back and forth between here and Ironcliff."

"There will, indeed. Kasri will be able to go home whenever she likes."

Herdwin looked at his soon-to-be forge mate, sitting back in her chair, looking exceedingly comfortable. "What do you say to that?"

Kasri smiled. "This is my home now."

Epilogue

WINTER 966 MC

(In the language of the Dwarves)

K asri's footsteps echoed on the marble floor. Her father, Thalgrun Stormhammer, sat on his throne, waving aside all those seeking his attention, his eyes on his only daughter. She halted before him, bowing reverentially.

"Kasri," he said. "I wondered when I might see you again."

"I came to speak with you, Father, although a conversation in private would be more appropriate."

"Nonsense. Whatever you want to say may be spoken in front of all assembled. Speak your mind, Daughter, and know I shall hold nothing against you."

"I come to renounce my position as successor."

The entire court went quiet.

"Renounce?" said the vard. "Whatever are you talking about?"

"I wish to forge with Herdwin Steelarm, master smith of

Wincaster. I know the guild has refused him entry, but I don't care. I will forge with him, and none can deny me."

"Good," her father replied.

"Good?" Kasri was at a loss for further words.

"It's about time you came to your senses."

"Did you not hear me, Father? I said I renounce my role as successor. You must find another Dwarf to succeed you to the Throne of Ironcliff."

"I shall do no such thing!"

Her face reddened. "You do not control me; I will forge whether or not you like it."

"As I would expect, but you are my chosen successor. Nothing changes my mind on that."

"But you said he wasn't worthy!"

"It was a test."

"A test? What kind of jest is this?"

"It is no jest, I assure you. A vard must be decisive, Kasri, and willing to stand up for what they believe in." He cast his gaze around the room. "There are many here who will disagree with your choice, but I assure you I am not amongst them. Your life is yours to live as you see fit. I only ask that, when the time comes, you return to Ironcliff to take your rightful place as vard."

"And Herdwin?"

"I assumed he'd accompany you, of course, but that's entirely up to him."

"I don't know what to say. You've taken me completely by surprise."

"You need say nothing for now, but you have much work ahead of you."

"I do?"

"Certainly," replied her father, "for you must decide who you will invite to your ceremony! Now, come. Sit by my side and regale me with tales of your adventures!"

REVIEW INTO THE FORGE

ON TO BOOK ELEVEN: GUARDIAN OF THE CROWN

If you liked *Into the Forge,* then *Temple Knight,* the first book in the *Power Ascending* series awaits.
START TEMPLE KNIGHT

Cast of Characters

People

IRONCLIFF
Agramath - Earth Mage, Master of Rock and Stone
Grimdal (Deceased) - Previous Vard
Kasri Ironheart - Daughter of Vard Thalgrun
Lord Graldur - Deputy Guildmaster, mining guild
Malrun Bronzefist - Master of Revels
Thalgrun Stormhammer - Vard

STONECASTLE
Belnik - Dwarf warrior, Gelion's company
Bremel (Deceased) - Great uncle of Herdwin, died in the mines of Stonecastle
Gelion Brightaxe - Cousin of Herdwin, Dwarf captain, husband to Margel
Golmar Hengesplitter - Engineer

Grennik Ironbeard - Guildmaster, smith's guild
Grolik - Dwarven warrior, Forlorn Tower
Herdwin Steelarm - Dwarven smith, spent years in
Wincaster, friend of Queen Anna
Kharzun (Deceased) - Past Vard
Khazad - Lord of the Stone, Dwarven Vard
Margel - Wife of Gelion
Naldurn Grimaxe - Blonde Dwarf from Stonecastle, fought
at Galburn's Ridge
Ragnus - Dwarf warrior, Gelion's company
Rotmir - Dwarven warrior, Forlorn Tower
Taldur - Dwarven warrior, Forlorn Tower
Thalbek - Dwarf warrior, Gelion's company

OTHERS
Albreda - Mistress (Witch) of the Whitewood, Earth Mage
Aldwin Fitzwilliam - Master smith, husband of Beverly
Fitzwilliam
Alric - Husband of Queen Anna of Merceria, heir to
Weldwyn
Anna - Queen of Merceria
Arandil Greycloak - Elven ruler of the Darkwood
Aubrey Brandon - Life Mage, Baroness of Hawksburg
Beverly Fitzwilliam "Redblade" - Knight Commander of the
Hound, daughter of Baron Fitzwilliam, married to Aldwin
Fitzwilliam
Darfal - Provincial warrior of Halvaria
Delsaran - Elf bard
Elariel - Elf maid, Last Hope Inn
Falcon - Proprietor of the Last Hope Inn

Gerald Matheson - Marshal of Merceria
Hugh Gardner - Sergeant, Army of Merceria
Kraloch - Orc shaman of the Black Arrows
Kythelia (Deceased) - Elf Necromancer
Melathandil - Dragon
Preston - Knight of the Hound, in service to the Queen of Merceria
Revy Bloom - Royal Life Mage
Richard 'Fitz' Fitzwilliam - Baron of Bodden, father of Beverly, uncle to Aubrey
Shalariel- Mistress of Thorolandrin
Telethial (Deceased) - Elf, daughter of Lord Arandil Greycloak
Valdarian - Halvarian truthseeker

PLACES
Forlorn Tower (Tower of Might) - Tower on route to Stonecastle
Galburn's Ridge - Capital of Norland
Ironcliff - Dwarven stronghold, northeast of Norland
Kharzun's Folly - Bridge spanning a ravine east of Stonecastle
Queen's Arms - Tavern near the Royal Palace in Wincaster
Stonecastle - Dwarven stronghold east of Wincaster
The Darkwood - Large forest, home of Elves
The Iron Ingot - Tavern in Stonecastle
Thorolandrin - Elven city within the Darkwood
Thunder Mountains - Near Ironcliffe
Wayward Wood - Home of the Wood Elves, south of Ironcliff

Wincaster - Capital of Merceria

THINGS

Battle of Redridge (962 MC) - Battle during the Mercerian civil war

Northern War - Name given to the recent war with Norland

Gundar - God of earth, creator of the Dwarves

Haldur - God of smiths and metalworking

Hearth Guard - Elite Dwarven company

Nature's Fury - Magic hammer used by Beverly Fitzwilliam

Stormhammer - Magic hammer used by Kasri Ironheart

Tauril - Goddess of the Wood and creator of the Elves

Vard - Dwarven term for a king or queen

Wood Elves - Cousins to High Elves, smaller stature

A Few Words From Paul

Into the Forge came about almost by accident. I'd been considering a story about Herdwin for quite some time, knowing it would involve him travelling back to Stonecastle, but the overall story arc eluded me. It wasn't until I introduced Kasri in *War of the Crown* that an idea took hold. She would accompany him on his trip, where they would encounter the Halvarian Empire. I even had an outline, but something was still missing.

Then along came *Triumph of the Crown*. I hadn't intended for these two characters to form such an attachment, it just happened, but that's when I knew *Into the Forge* would be about the story of their journey together.

It also occurred to me that such a tale would make an interesting song, and thus I introduced an Elven bard, as well as something new: two verses of poetry to begin each chapter. This tale was a delight to write, and I finished it in a relatively short period, but it ranks among my favourite short stories. Well, I say short, but it's really a novel.

I'm not done with Herdwin and Kasri yet. Their story continues in *Guardian of the Crown*, Book 11 of the Heir to the Crown series.

I must thank my wife, Carol, for her support and for helping me flesh out the storyline. It's because of her that I can concentrate on the task of writing rather than marketing, editing, and everything else that authors need to do these days. She is, as the Dwarves say, my forge mate, and I am delighted to be taking this journey with her.

I would also like to thank my daughters, Christie Bennett, Stephanie Sandrock, and Amanda Bennett, for their continued encouragement. Moral support was also provided by Brad Aitken, Stephen Brown and the memory of Jeffrey Parker, who brought the world of Merceria to life in the first place.

I should also like to thank my BETA team for their tireless input and their fantastic feedback, so thank you: Rachel Deibler, Michael Rhew, Phyllis Simpson, Don Hinckley, Charles Mohapel, Debra Reeves, Mitchell Schneidkraut, Susan Young, Joanna Smith, Keven Hutchinson, and Anna Ostberg

Last but not least, I must thank you, the reader, without whom these stories would never see the light of day. Your comments and encouragement inspire me to continue with these tales.

About the Author

Paul J Bennett (b. 1961) emigrated from England to Canada in 1967. His father served in the British Royal Navy, and his mother worked for the BBC in London. As a young man, Paul followed in his father's footsteps, joining the Canadian Armed Forces in 1983. He is married to Carol Bennett and has three daughters who are all creative in their own right.

Paul's interest in writing started in his teen years when he discovered the roleplaying game, Dungeons & Dragons (D & D). What attracted him to this new hobby was the creativity it required; the need to create realms, worlds and adventures that pulled the gamers into his stories.

In his 30's, Paul started to dabble in designing his own roleplaying system, using the Peninsular War in Portugal as his backdrop. His regular gaming group were willing victims, er, participants in helping to playtest this new system. A few years later, he added additional settings to his game, including Science Fiction, Post-Apocalyptic, World War II, and the all-important Fantasy Realm where his stories take place.

The beginnings of his first book 'Servant to the Crown' originated over five years ago when he began running a new fantasy campaign. For the world that the Kingdom of Merceria is in, he ran his adventures like a TV show, with seasons that each had twelve episodes, and an overarching plot. When the campaign ended, he knew all the characters, what they had to accomplish, what needed to happen to move the plot along, and it was this that inspired to sit down to write his first novel.

Paul now has four series based in his fantasy world of Eiddenwerthe, and is looking forward to sharing many more books with his readers over the coming years.